"I used to hero-worship you," Storm found herself saying haltingly.

"Then all at once things changed," Luke replied. "I'm here for you, Storm. Any chance we could start again?"

"No, I just can't," she said in a passion. "Too many years have gone by."

"What are you  you so frightened of ...

"Such arroganc ... "I'm not fright ... ve to do to prove it?" She stood there in an attitude of defiance he had witnessed countless times over.

"Why don't you let me show you?"

"Don't you dare touch me, Luke," she warned.

He gave a challenging shake of his head. "I'm genuinely amazed I haven't tried it before. For years you were too young, but you're old enough now."

Margaret Way takes great pleasure in her work and works hard at her pleasure. She enjoys tearing off to the beach with her family at weekends, loves haunting galleries and auctions and is completely given over to French champagne "for every possible joyous occasion." She was born and educated in the river city of Brisbane, Australia, and now lives within sight and sound of beautiful Moreton Bay.

Books by Margaret Way

Don't miss any of our special offers. Write to us at the following address for information on our newest releases.

Harlequin Reader Service
U.S.: 3010 Walden Ave., P.O. Box 1325, Buffalo, NY 14269
Canadian: P.O. Box 609, Fort Erie, Ont. L2A 5X3

MARGARET WAY

Outback Fire

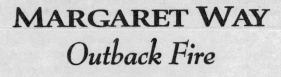

HARLEQUIN®

TORONTO • NEW YORK • LONDON
AMSTERDAM • PARIS • SYDNEY • HAMBURG
STOCKHOLM • ATHENS • TOKYO • MILAN • MADRID
PRAGUE • WARSAW • BUDAPEST • AUCKLAND

ISBN 0-373-03679-5

OUTBACK FIRE

First North American Publication 2001.

Copyright © 2001 Margaret Way, Pty., Ltd.

Visit us at www.eHarlequin.com

Printed in U.S.A.

PROLOGUE

THEY rode out at dawn. Their mission was specific. To hunt down "Psycho" the wild bull camel that was harassing the herd and attacking anybody unfortunate enough to come on it unawares. The situation had become so dangerous it was now necessary to kill the beast. Only a few days before one of the stockmen mustering clean skins on the desert fringe had encountered the raging animal and paid the price. Psycho had attacked without provocation kicking the stockman in the chest. The consequences had been serious. The man had to be airlifted to hospital and was still in a critical condition. He would have been dead only for the arrival of three of his mates who had startled the ferocious beast into slewing off.

When the rogue came on season, for it was the male camel instead of the female that came on heat, Psycho would pose even more of a threat. He had a fearful reputation for attacking other male camels with passionate fury, his strength and wildness driving them away to leave him with a harem usually twenty or more females he jealously guarded and impregnated.

Of recent times Psycho had taken to making openmouthed dives at the tribal people who crisscrossed the station on walkabout. McFarlane had been informed of the attacks. His people were frightened and wanted protection.

Camels weren't indigenous to Australia. They and their Afghan handlers had been imported into the country in the early days of settlement to transport goods all over the dry trackless regions of the Outback; camels were ideal beasts of burden in just such conditions. Their wild descendants, some quarter of a million and they lived several decades, were a dreadful menace. They roamed the desert from one end to the other doing considerable damage to the fragile environment. McFarlane tolerated them. By now they were part of the Outback and there was a certain romance to the sight of them silhouetted on top of a sand dune at sunset. Unfortunately the time had come for Psycho to be destroyed before he turned killer.

Six of them made up the party that morning. McFarlane, his overseer, Chas Branagan, Garry Dingo, the station's finest tracker, two of his best stockmen and the boy, Luke. Fourteen years old but already judged by the others to be a man. The boy stood six feet, a superb athlete, with an excellent head on his shoulders. He was a fine shot, a talent he had been born with, as well as having extraordinary endurance for his age. In fact he was well on his way to becoming a consummate bushman like his father, Chas. He had the same remarkable sight, hearing and sense of smell. Skills that would be needed on the hunt.

McFarlane realised he had become very fond of the boy. Indeed he was coming to look on him as the son he might have had. The tragedy was his wife; the one woman he had ever truly loved had died in childbirth leaving him with the precious legacy of a daughter. His beautiful Storm. While her mother slipped prematurely out of life, Storm had come into the world at the height of one of the fiercest tempests that had ever passed over his land.

Tragedy and triumph. Sometimes the two went hand in hand. Like Storm and high drama. Storm had never been an easy child. Tempestuous and outspoken she spent her young life rebelling against his dictates when he had only put them in place to protect her. Freedom was what she wanted. Total freedom. The right to roam the station at will. "Like Luke does." That was the catch cry "Like Luke does."

There were always outbursts against Luke. Big flare-ups of jealousy and resentment.

"You treat him like a son! He's *not* your son. He's *not* my brother."

How many times had he heard that? Storm fought his affection for Luke every step of the way. She overplayed her little princess and the pauper act most times the two of them were together. Luke being Luke, was gentle and tolerant with her, unfazed by her histrionics.

As for Storm, the light of his life, didn't she know her father adored her? When Storm was sweet, she was very, very sweet, irresistible like her mother. If she'd had her way she'd have joined them this morning. Imagine! A girl barely twelve, even if she could ride all day. Storm couldn't accept the confines of her femininity. She lived in a man's world and she wasn't about to come to terms with it. His difficult little Storm. How could it be otherwise? This was a child reared without a mother's gentling touch.

They skirted around the lignum that rose up like jungle walls, the party dividing up as they rode into the desert, ringed by heat waves that danced in the blinding glare. No tracks so far but then they had to contend with the rising wind that wiped them out almost as soon as they were made. Such a place of desolation this no man's land! The great flights of budgerigar that flashed green and gold overhead and the marauding hawks were almost the only living things. The grazing cattle had stripped the perennial cover from the slopes here and the blood-red sand moved at will.

Sand and spinifex.

This year of drought, even the spinifex wasn't so dense. Other years it covered the sand like a bright golden carpet.

After two hours or more of fruitless search the party broke up, frustrated but not willing to give up. Psycho should have been spottable but he wasn't. Wild animals had a way of disappearing into the landscape. Chas and two of the stockmen took off for the low eroded foothills, shimmering in the quicksilver light of the mirage. McFarlane, Luke and Matt, the other stockman, worked the undulating dunes, so red they were alight. It was getting hotter and hotter, the sun scorching out of a cloudless blue sky. So hot in fact McFarlane knew he was losing concentration. Not yet fifty he had lived a hard, dangerous life, and it was taking its toll. Broken ribs, a bad leg injury years back in Vietnam that still gave him a lot of pain especially if he was too long in the saddle. A tired man became careless. Matt had dropped back, skirting the mounds of dried up springs. He rode ahead with Luke a few feet from his shoulder.

Everything was silence. Infinity. The blood-red dunes ran on forever in great parallel waves; the tall seed stems of the spinifex called up glittering aboriginal spears. Nothing to signal the presence of the camel as it watched them, its shaggy, dull ginger coat an excellent camouflage. It stood within its crude shelter of desert acacias, its dark crested humped outline hidden by the thick gnarled trunks and weight of branches. McFarlane saw the wild camel as his quarry. Psycho in a particularly vicious mood saw McFarlane as his.

With extraordinary cunning the rogue camel waited for the optimum moment to break cover. It gathered itself for the charge then galloped directly at McFarlane with terrifying speed, its hump grown massive over the years, swaying, drumming through its nostrils its blind rage at the threat to its territory. In the crystal clear air of the desert the sound was deafening, travelling far. McFarlane slumped half sideways in the saddle trying to ease the pain in his leg, felt the hairs at the back of his neck stand up. For an instant he was deadly afraid then he wheeled his horse sharply but that stout hearted animal quailed in the face of the camel's blazing charge. It reared then thundered to the ground throwing the unsettled McFarlane out of the saddle and onto the sun-baked earth.

The boy, Luke, looked on in horror, a cry caught in his throat. For a split second he was frozen, then all thoughts of his own safety left him. He was ice cool, bracing himself for what lay ahead. This wasn't anything he couldn't handle. Every lost second almost certainly meant tragedy. There was only time for one shot. It had to be perfect. Clean. Humane. Conclusive.

Eye to the sight, finger on the trigger Luke waited…waited…his handsome young face strong and resolute. He was already beginning to squeeze the trigger. The camel was slobbering hugely, saturated in foaming fury. Its rank smell pervaded the air.

The shot cracked away echoing across the desert and bouncing off the boulders strewn about like giants' marbles. The camel died in mid-flight. It crashed to the ground, thrashed for an aftermoment then rolled motionless to one side, its body making a deep impression in the sand.

Urgently Luke dismounted and rushed to McFarlane's prone figure. Perfectly in control one minute, he was now uncertain. Anxiously he went down on one knee, eyes checking. "Mr. McFarlane?" he cried hoarsely. Every last man, woman and child on the vast station depended on this man. To many of them he was their guardian.

McFarlane lay for a moment, racked in pain and panting, thick dark hair and deeply tanned skin clogged with red dust, his grey akubra lying a foot away. Eventually, with air in his lungs, he managed a quiet "I'm fine, boy. Fine. No need to worry. That was a close one."

Luke nodded, shoving his hat to the back of his dark auburn head. "Any closer and you'd have been trampled." Now the danger was over, his voice broke with emotion.

"No way! Not with you around. You're a man and I'm proud of you."

McFarlane heaved himself into a sitting position, wincing as he reached for his wide-brimmed hat. He settled it on his head, then allowed the boy to help him up. A fine boy. Brave and loyal. "I guess you could say you saved my life," McFarlane pronounced, his deep voice showing an answering emotion. He rested one large, strong hand on the boy's shoulder. "You stood your ground in the face of fear. I promise you I won't forget it."

The colour flushed into the boy's dark cheeks. He murmured something inaudible. Nevertheless it was one of those moments in life that are never forgotten.

CHAPTER ONE

By the time they finished yarding the brumbies every crinkle, every crevice of his face was ingrained with red dust. After a day of intense heat and real feats of riding through the rough country Luke was desperate for a shower and a long cold beer. He was due up at the homestead this evening for dinner and a game of chess. The Major loved his chess. He loved the right company. They were both accomplished players and they had long enjoyed an easy companionable relationship.

Nowadays Athol McFarlane, for so long a lion of a man, was going downhill right in front of the younger man's eyes. It deeply pained him. After the deaths of his parents Athol was all he had. He owed everything to the Major. Everyone on the station called him that. A carryover from his early days as a much decorated army officer in Vietnam. It was a term of affection now. No one was sure who started it. It certainly hadn't been Athol McFarlane. Those were the days he didn't care to talk about. *Ever*. Still only in his early sixties the Major had ongoing problems with his leg, an injury he had sustained in the war. What exactly those problems were, Luke never could find out, and he sure as hell had tried, but the Major didn't like to talk about his state of health although it was obvious to everyone who cared about him that he was deteriorating. And Luke suspected in constant pain, though there was never a word of complaint. The only complaint that passed the Major's lips were: "When is Storm coming home?"

He knew the old man missed her terribly. He missed

11

her, too. Sometimes he thought like a hole in the head. Other times like a hole in the heart. He never could contend with his feelings about Storm. He only knew it didn't pay to delve too deeply. She was beautiful. He had a vision of her out riding, cloud of sable hair flying—she hated wearing a hat even in the intense heat—not that it had affected her flawless ivory complexion, green cat's eyes sparkling with life and health.

He knew she was clever. She designed and made exclusive jewellery that sold as far away as New York. Necklaces, pendants, bangles, rings. You name it. And the beautiful people flew from all over just to have a piece designed by Storm McFarlane. Not bad to have an enviable reputation at twenty-seven. No husband. Two fiancés that never managed to get her to the altar. High time she was married, the Major said. He wanted to set eyes on his grandchildren before he died. So far Storm hadn't obliged. What was she waiting for? Superman? Only a rare man could satisfy her, he thought with black humour. Storm always had been damned near impossible to please. Certainly he had never succeeded except for those odd times when they acknowledged a bond. More than a bond. God knows what it was.

When he reached the comfortable overseer's bungalow that had once housed his small happy family, Luke went straight to the bathroom, stripped off his dusty clothes and ran a warm shower. After such a day, it took a while to feel completely clean. He had to soap his hair as well to rid it of the dust, then he allowed the water to run cold, luxuriating in the blessed sensation of feeling cool. Here he was twenty-nine and one of the greatest things in life was a shower!

My God!

Not that he hadn't had his own little romantic flutters. A few months of thinking maybe this is it, then the initial burst of interest and excitement drained away like the water in a clay pan. A few of his ex-girlfriends still hung in there. That was the amazing thing. He hadn't really lost a one. Carla was the most persistent without a doubt. He really liked Carla. She was good company, good-looking and she was good in bed. What the hell was the matter with him? Like Storm it was high time he was married. Deep inside he mourned the loss of his family. He had to make a family for himself. With the right woman. But who? A woman like Storm, who never failed to move and outrage him was out of the question. Storm McFarlane was trouble with a capital *T*.

Luke towelled himself off and slicked back his hair. Now and again he caught glimpses of his father in his mirrored reflection—the high cheekbones, the set of the eyes and mouth. But his colouring was purely his mother's. Though the worst of the pain had banked down to liveable he missed his parents every day of his life. He remembered as though it were yesterday getting the message to go to the headmaster's office. He sensed it was something important but never in a million years did he expect to see the Major, handsome and dignified seated in the headmaster's study.

The Major had come personally to break the terrible news. His parents had been killed in a three-car collision driving back from Alice Springs. One of the cars driven by a tourist was found to have been travelling on the wrong side of the road. His parents had been in the wrong place at the wrong time. He was then fifteen years old and a boarder at one of the country's most prestigious private schools. His parents had been determined he would have a good education but they could never have afforded *that* particular school with its proud tradition, splendid amenities and brilliant alumni that read like a Who's Who. The

Major had seen to it. Wouldn't take no for an answer. Wore Luke's dad down.

After the accident the Major had flown Luke and Storm back to the station for the funeral. Storm had insisted she be picked up from her boarding school so she could be there. Although her hang-ups had always centred on Luke she had been great friends with his mother and father. Particularly his mother who thought the world of "the little princess."

As a mark of deep respect his parents had actually been buried in the McFarlane family cemetery on Sanctuary Hill, some five kilometres from the homestead. He remembered how Storm had stood white-faced beside him holding his hand. He remembered how she had given him real comfort for once, hostilities set aside. He hadn't forgotten. Although Storm had to return to school he had stayed up at the Big House with the Major trying to master his terrible grief, but never coming to terms with it, then he, too, had to return to boarding school. After that, university.

Luke had graduated from college with an OP1, the top score, something else that had set Storm off. She had scored an excellent OP3. After that, the Major insisted he, along with Storm, go on to higher education which after all he had wanted himself. Luke'd worked hard and made the Major proud, picking up an honours degree in Economics. He'd been free to choose his own life after that but all he had ever wanted was to be a cattleman like his dad. Running a huge operation was big business these days, not just learning the game. Luke revelled in Outback life. It was in his blood and he had never felt truly at home in the city. He'd told the Major this in a long discussion. It was then the Major had confounded him by offering him his father's old job. Overseer of Winding River Station. A top job with big responsibilities. The two outstations now came under his jurisdiction.

These days he was the Major's right hand man. Visitors to the station, those not in the know, often mistook him for McFarlane's son. His rise had been meteoric but no one in a tough competitive world had ever questioned his ability. To prove it the Major was leaving more and more to him to the point where he was virtually running the whole operation.

Dressed in a clean shirt and jeans he walked up to the Big House pausing outside to admire it. He always did. It was a magnificent old house completed in the late 1870s by Ian Essex McFarlane a wealthy pastoralist who had come from the colony of New South Wales to take up this vast holding in South West Queensland. The house had been planned on a grand scale, all the more extraordinary for its remote desert setting, two storeyed, built of warm golden sandstone with a slate roof, its deep verandahs supported by slender white pillars with unusual lotus capitals forming a striking colonnade, the upper verandahs encased in white wrought-iron lace with very attractive fretwork. Semicircular stone steps led to the deeply recessed front door and he took them two at a time, passing into the spacious entrance hall its parqueted floor strewn with oriental rugs. Noni Mercer, the housekeeper, came out to greet him, smiling up into his face. "Hi there, Luke. Hot old day!"

"You want to try running down brumbies," he answered, returning her smile. Noni was a thoroughly nice woman. He was fond of her and had good reason to be. In her late fifties, short and compact, with a great heart, she had a bubble of grey curls and contrasting snapping dark eyes. "I have to tell you, Noni, I'm ready for your cooking."

"Aren't you always!" Noni blushed with pleasure. She ran her eyes appreciatively over Luke's rangy figure. He stood straight and tall, superbly built, a few inches over six feet. She had watched him grow up. Watched him turn into this almost unbelievably handsome young man with hair like a dark flame and those miraculous blue eyes. His lovely little mother, Rose, God rest her soul, had had just that marvellous colouring.

Noni had a very soft spot for Luke Branagan who never once used his high standing with the Major for his own gain. Straight as a die was Luke. How he and Storm weren't the greatest friends Noni could never understand. She had an idea Luke secretly carried a torch for the tempestuous Storm, though he would never let on, even under torture. Sadly, in Noni's opinion, and she cared deeply for Storm, that young woman had her feet set on a different path. Yet when she saw them together? Noni heaved a soft sigh, which made Luke dip his handsome head to look into her eyes.

"What's up?"

For such a big strong, dynamic guy Luke was in touch with women's feelings. "Nothing, dear," Noni evaded, then felt compelled to burst out with what was on her mind. "When is Storm coming home?"

His handsome face tautened. "Hell, Noni, why ask me? I'm not one of Storm's favourite people. You know that."

"She's been running with that for a long time," Noni gruffly scoffed. "Personally I don't think it's true."

"Well she sure doesn't *love* me," Luke's vibrant voice deepened. "And she doesn't confide in me, either."

"More's the pity!" Noni regretted. "The Major hasn't been terribly well today, but he's so looking forward to seeing you. You're not far off the son he never had."

"Maybe that's the problem, Noni," Luke's expression turned a shade bleak. "Storm hates to see it that way."

Noni couldn't do other than nod her agreement. "I just wish she'd come home." She turned her head quickly as slow, heavy footsteps sounded along the upper gallery. "That will be the Major now," she said softly. "I know Storm has a busy life. She's so successful and that's wonderful. She always was a clever little thing. Remember how she used to collect all those little bits of opal and quartz around the station?"

Luke's handsome mouth compressed. "I distinctly remember finding a lot of it for her. She was in heaven when the Major used to organize those prospecting trips to the gemfields for us. I made quite a few finds myself but I always handed them over to Storm."

"You would," Noni said. For all her tantrums Luke had always been honey-sweet to that little girl. Sweet and calm and understanding. Maybe he should have told her off. He was well capable of telling off the toughest and the roughest.

"Agate, amethyst, carnelian, garnet, sapphire, topaz, beryl," Luke was saying, his brilliant blue eyes reflective. "That's what started her off on her career. The Major always encouraged her. Now she's getting to be a big name."

"It's marvellous," Noni a recipient of several beautiful little pieces, smiled. "Storm is delighted when people fall in love with her work."

"She's not happy with guys falling in love with her," Luke commented dryly. "Two fiancés to date. Neither could get her to the altar."

"You're not married, either," Noni pointed out slyly. "You're quite a pair!" Personally she thought each had ruined relationships for the other.

As they were speaking Athol McFarlane appeared at the top of the central staircase then came very slowly down towards them. He was leaning very heavily on his stick but Luke and Noni knew better than to go to his assistance. The Major scorned help. He was independent to a fault.

"Well, Luke," he boomed, and his gaunt face lit up. "Come tell me all about your day. Noni has been fussing for hours lining up all the things you like to eat."

"She spoils me," Luke grinned, knowing it was true.

"And you're worth every bit of it." The Major nodded his thatched grey head that once had had Storm's raven sheen. "You've been the greatest help to me these past years. Devotion and dedication. Not a lot of men are as capable of it as you, son. You keep bringing your dad to mind. A splendid man. Not that I had any illusions he wouldn't have wanted to strike out for himself one day. With *my* blessing, mind, but that was not to be." Athol McFarlane's expression grew grave and introspective. "Come along now into the study. You might have to fly over to Kingston at the end of the week. About time to pay them a surprise visit. Noni will let us know when dinner is ready."

"Will do, Major," Noni gave a comic little salute and made off for the kitchen, thanking God Luke was around to ease the Major's pain and loneliness.

Above the fireplace in the Major's book-and-trophy-lined study hung a painting of Storm. It had been commissioned on the eve of her twenty-first birthday. He found himself looking up at it with a brooding silence. No lavish ball gown for Storm. No deep *décolletage* that would have shown off her beautiful shoulders and breasts. But the painting, like Storm, compelled attention. She was wearing riding clothes, white silk shirt and close-fitting beige mole-skins, a fancy belt with a heavy silver-and-opal studded buckle she had designed herself around her narrow waist. Her long black hair was blowing free, her head slightly profiled, skin luminous, her almond-shaped eyes the same rich emerald-green as the bandanna that was knotted carelessly around her throat. One beautiful long-fingered hand was on her hip, and the other clasped a white akubra with a wide snakeskin band. How many times had he seen her stand like that? Maybe a thousand. As a background the artist had used the wonderful colourations of the desert; the cloudless cobalt-blue sky, the purple hills, the gleaming gold of the spinifex dotting the red ochre plains. The setting lent the painting a kind of monumentality. The young woman up there looked so vivid, so real he had the sense she could very easily step from the frame.

Into his arms?

And then?

He never saw it without getting an erotic charge. He was under no illusion Storm couldn't move him powerfully. Nothing easy or relaxed about it. Blinding pleasure and sometimes more than its fair share of sexual hostility.

The Major, observing Luke quietly but intently, took his usual seat waiting for the young man to join him. "Could I ask you something very personal, Luke," Athol McFarlane queried, meeting that direct sapphire gaze.

"Sure, Major, as long as you leave Storm out of it," Luke returned deadpan.

McFarlane laughed. "What impresses me most about you two is neither of you can find anyone else while the other's around."

Luke, taken by surprise, didn't answer immediately. "You're suggesting a love-hate?"

"More often than not it's Storm waging the war," McFarlane answered ruefully. "I would have thought she'd be long over it by now."

"She'll never be over it," Luke answered, a mite tightly.

"I can't accept that," the Major growled. "I want to see her, Luke." It came out far more plaintively than he ever intended.

Luke stared across the table, perturbed by the Major's tone. "What's up? What's the matter? I wish you'd confide in me."

"Nothing to confide," McFarlane lied. He wanted desperately to tell Luke he was dying but he couldn't. He wouldn't even tell Storm. "I'm just feeling tired and old and lonely except for you," he evaded. "You're my adopted son, Luke. You know that."

"If there was anything badly wrong you'd tell me?" There was a serious almost stern expression in Luke's face.

"Sure I would." McFarlane tried to lighten that gaze.

"Why don't I believe that? I'm here to help you, Major."

The Major responded by grasping Luke's forearm. "Don't you think I know that, son? But it's four months at least since Storm was here."

Four months, one week and three days. "She leads a full life," Luke pointed out. "Even I've picked up the magazines Noni leaves lying around the place. She's beautiful, gifted, she has a fine family name. It's only to be expected she'd get invited everywhere. And she has her work. Her commissions."

"She could do them here." The Major's heavy eyebrows drew together. "I've offered many times to convert a couple of rooms into a studio, workshop, whatever she wants. God knows there are enough rooms empty."

"Have you told her how you feel?" Luke asked.

McFarlane sighed. "Yes." It wasn't strictly true. He always played hardy when she rang.

"And she *still* won't come?" It was hard to keep the censure out of his voice. Storm had plenty of time for parties and all the social functions.

"Maybe I haven't asked the right way." McFarlane dropped his gaze evasively, sighing heavily.

"You must know it's on account of *me*."

"I don't accept that, Luke." McFarlane shook his head.

"I think you might *have* to, Major," Luke countered knowing the Major had been living with the fiction one day he and Storm would get together. God, could you believe it? "Storm has always seen me as the usurper," he added with quiet force, opening up his own wounds.

"Rubbish! That's irrational." The Major's protest was overloud.

"Aren't human beings irrational when their deepest emotions are involved?" Luke held the Major's gaze until he blinked.

"You're a man of integrity, Luke," McFarlane said. "Storm knows that in her deepest being."

Luke's expression became sombre as he studied the other man's gaunt face, thin body and arms. "Would you like me to go to Sydney and fetch her?"

McFarlane looked up quickly. "You're far too busy to do that," he protested but his face brightened and he squared his shoulders.

"Everything is in hand," Luke pointed out. "I've got Sandy well trained. He can stand in for me for a day of two. Of course if you want me to check out Kingston?" Luke referred to a Winding River's outstation.

"It can wait," McFarlane said without a second thought.

"Actually it *can*. I've got the situation sorted out. Webb was the troublemaker."

McFarlane scarcely heard, his voice picking up strength.

"When will you go?" Luke studied him. It sounded as if time was of the essence.

"When would you want me to go?" Luke watched him carefully, evaluating the change.

"What about Friday?"

The day after tomorrow. Luke's mind worked overtime. The Major hid his desperation well but Luke sensed, no *knew,* there was something terribly wrong. He wished he could talk to Tom Skinner, the Major's doctor. Get things straight, but the Major would never forgive him for going behind his back. He had tried to get something out of Tom, to little avail. Whatever the true state of McFarlane's health the file was confidential. But there was the evidence of his own eyes. The Major was a sick man. He knew it. Storm knew it. Where the hell was she? Surely her concern for her father would outweigh every other consideration? Her long-running cold war with him?

"So?" McFarlane asked as the young man opposite him fell silent.

"No problem!" Luke flashed his white smile. The smile everyone waited for. "I won't let Storm know I'm coming in case she jumps town, though I will check to see she's in residence."

"What about young Carla?" the Major suddenly side-tracked.

"You could give me a clue?" Luke drawled, not wanting to discuss Carla.

"Dammit, Luke, you know what I mean. You and Carla used to be close. Is it still on?"

Luke picked up a paperweight and palmed it. "On and off. Carla and I are friends." He set the crystal paperweight down.

'You're a darn sight more to her than that, my boy," the Major scoffed. "I've got eyes. The girl is head over heels in love with you. Her dad would be thrilled to have you for a son-in-law. Like me he only has a daughter to inherit."

Luke, a generation younger, was very much attuned to women's issues. "Don't underestimate Carla," he said. "She's got a good head on her shoulders. She knows the business as well as her dad. She could take over."

The Major shrugged. "It's too hard a life for a woman, Luke. You know that. It's tough, dangerous and you want a man as boss. Even Storm realises that. Accidents happen all the time around stations especially remote ones like ours. What woman is willing to put herself through that? I'm only trying to find out what the position is with you and Carla."

"Why exactly?" Luke asked, with a look of dry humour.

The Major blew up. "Hell, son, you're as close-lipped as I am. I care about you, that's why. I like Carla, too. She's a smart girl and a looker but I think you can do better."

"Such as Storm?" Luke asked directly.

"Surely you can understand that," McFarlane asked. "Your lives are entwined. No matter what, there's that bond. Nothing in this world would make me happier than to see you and Storm together."

Luke gave a hollow laugh, his eyes drawn to Storm's portrait. "It would take an eternity for Storm and I to patch up our differences," he said thinking Storm's childhood had been damaged by the desperate need to be the only one in her father's life. She should have had brothers and sisters. She should have had *anyone*, except him. In his own way, without warning, the Major had set them both up.

Now the Major was saying very seriously, "I know

Storm has given you a rough time—and you've let her. She's the only one who could get away with it, but she knows your worth. She *knows,* Luke, even if it would kill her to admit it.''

"My thoughts exactly," Luke quipped. "It's just a dream of yours, Major. An impossible dream."

"But you care about her?" McFarlane challenged. "You can't look me in the eye and tell me you don't. I know you too well."

"Then you'd know I would never waste time wanting a woman who didn't want me," Luke said emphatically. What the hell else was he doing if not that?

"Just bring her home, Luke," McFarlane begged with overwhelming intensity. "That's all I ask. If there's a God in his heaven he'll make things come right."

CHAPTER TWO

IT WAS getting on towards late afternoon before he touched down at Sydney's light aircraft terminal taking a cab into the city where he booked into a hotel. Storm herself had rung her father only the night before, in the course of the conversation letting it be known she wasn't going out of town that weekend. She was to be chief bridesmaid to Sara Lambert, a young woman the Major knew from her occasional visits to the station. Luke knew Sara, too. At one stage she'd had quite a crush on him that mercifully passed. So with any luck he would find Storm at home. Or if she did happen to go out for the evening, which he was sure she would, he would sit it out until she arrived back. In a curious way he realised he was elated at the thought of seeing her again. A good idea to check the hype now. Storm could be in one of her moods. Moods or not he was certain of one thing. This time she was coming back with him before something bad happened.

When he arrived at her seriously up-market apartment block he had no difficulty getting past security. The man at the desk knew him after seeing him a few times in company with Storm and the Major. In fact the man appeared to think he was Storm's brother.

"Go right up, Mr. McFarlane," he said breezily. "I saw Miss McFarlane come in a couple of hours ago. Didn't see her go out, though I've been away from the desk on and off."

He waved his thanks and moved towards the lift amus-

25

ing himself by thinking Storm most probably would be
overjoyed to see him.

As it turned out Storm wasn't in but a very smart-
looking older woman dressed in a blue suit emerged from
the adjoining apartment to tell him Storm had left for a
party at the Drysdales.

"You know them?" She must have been bored because
she looked as if she was ready for a chat.

"Heard of them certainly," he replied. Every year the
Drysdales made The Rich List. "I'm here on an errand for
Storm's father." He smiled.

"Then you'll be waiting a long time," the woman said
almost flirtatiously. "Those parties go on all night. Then
there's Sara Lambert's wedding tomorrow."

"Yes, I know Sara," he said, unaware he was frowning.

"Look here, why don't you simply turn up?" the
woman said. "I'm sure the Drysdales won't mind. Not if
you're a friend of Storm's. They adore her."

"Who doesn't?" he said with the faintest edge of irony.

"You know Storm obviously." The woman's bright
eyes were agog.

"I grew up with her." He told her casually, then lest
she got the wrong impression: "I'm the overseer on the
McFarlane station, Winding River."

The woman stared at him as if transfixed. "Really? It
must keep you very busy?"

"It does. I don't have a lot of time. I should fly back
tomorrow. Sunday by the latest."

"So go along to the party," the woman suggested, sens-
ing his urgency.

"What, in this?" He pulled at the sleeve of his leather
bomber jacket.

"My dear, you look *marvellous*," the woman breathed
and gave him the address.

The Drysdale mansion was right on Sydney harbour, which was to say on one of the most beautiful sites in the world. The imposing Italianate-style house with matching landscape grounds was ablaze with lights. There again he had no difficulty in gaining entrance. Like a gift from heaven, Sara Lambert, Storm's friend, had been invited to the party. They caught sight of each other as they approached the massive wrought-iron gates, open but flanked either side by attendants to vet the guests.

No male was dressed casually as he was. They either wore dinner jackets or well-tailored suits. Sara didn't appear to take much note of that. She rushed to his side, grabbing hold of his arm.

"Why Luke!" she carolled. "How lovely to see you! It's been ages and ages."

"Sara." He bent to brush her flushed cheek. "Your big day tomorrow. I wish you every happiness."

She beamed up at him, a very attractive blonde with sky-blue eyes. "I'd have sent you an invitation only you might have put me off going through with it," she said roguishly. "Only fooling. I love my Michael."

"I'm sure you do."

"Storm didn't tell me you were coming tonight?" She took his arm affectionately, as though they were the greatest of friends.

"Actually, Sara, she doesn't know."

The blue eyes rounded. "You can't be serious?"

"I'm absolutely serious. I'm here on behalf of her father. Literally a flying visit. The Major's not well."

"Oh!" Sara kept moving toward the gates where an attendant smiled and nodded to her then let them through. Easy as that! "I'm so sorry. I do know the Major has ongoing problems with his leg. Storm keeps me informed. A lovely man, the Major."

"I think so."

"And he thinks the world of you," Sara told him warmly.

"Unlike Storm," he said in an easy, languid drawl that masked a lot of hurt.

Sara laughed. "Maybe she's in denial. You two go back a long way."

"That we do." He left it at that.

Moving in line, they were almost at the front door: Luke without an invitation, Sara waving to other couples who had not yet worked their way into the house.

"I really don't think I should go in, Sara," he said. "If you wouldn't mind telling Storm I'm here? I'd like to speak to her for a few moments, then I'll be off."

"Oh for God's sake, stay!" Sara turned up her face to him, tightening her hold on his arm. "You're going to have to tell me what's been happening in your life. How's your girlfriend, Carla?"

"She's fine. I won't go in, Sara," he said firmly. "Apart from the fact I wasn't invited, I don't look the part." Not that he cared but he was old-fashioned enough not to want to gate-crash.

For an instant there was the same old hero worship in Sara's tone. "You look terrific! Like an ad for Calvin Klein. Great jeans and a cool leather jacket go anywhere."

Despite his wishes they were somehow through the grand double doors urged on by the press of guests to the rear. The entrance hall to his eyes was overly resplendent, more like the foyer of some sumptuous European hotel. Huge, even allowing for the swirl of laughing, chattering guests, all beautifully dressed, the women flashing spectacular jewellery. He presumed the handsome middle-aged couple in the centre were the Drysdales; something Sara immediately confirmed.

He moved back, to one side, taking Sara with him. "If you could just find Storm. I'd appreciate it."

Sara all but ignored him. "Don't you want to meet Stephanie and Gill?" she asked.

"Oh God! I think I'm about to," he said, watching the hosts break away from their other guests and walk towards them, looking highly interested.

"Sara, darling!" Stephanie Drysdale cried.

Lots of Euro kisses.

"This is Luke," Sara offered brightly. "Luke Branagan. He's Athol McFarlane's right hand man. Storm's father."

"Of course!" The hosts, husband and wife started to beam. Handshakes all round.

"Forgive me for gate-crashing your party," Luke smiled, "if only momentarily. I'm in Sydney to see Storm. I have a message for her from her father. It won't take long but it's important. Hence the flying visit. I'm needed back on the station. The Major hasn't been well."

"Nothing serious I hope?" Stephanie Drysdale asked, waiting on the answer.

"His health is a matter of concern, Mrs. Drysdale," he said.

"Well we must get Storm for you." Stephanie Drysdale turned to her husband. "Gill, why don't you show Mr. Branagan into the study while I find Storm. You'll want to be private." She hesitated a moment. "Are you going on anywhere else this evening, Mr. Branagan?" she asked.

"Luke, please." He gave her a smile. "I might catch a movie while I'm in town."

"Goodness! In that case we'd love you to stay." She flashed a glance at her husband, who nodded his handsome head in agreement. Sara, too, smiled excitedly.

"I'm not exactly dressed for the occasion," he pointed out amusedly, glancing down at his jeans and high boots.

"Don't worry about that. You look fine." Actually
Stephanie Drysdale was thinking she had never seen a man
looking so utterly divine.

Gilbert Drysdale led him off to the study while his wife
and Sara went in search of Storm. Guests were wandering
around everywhere, champagne glasses in hand, laughing,
talking, relaxed. They continued through one of the opu-
lent reception rooms along a corridor until they came to
the darkened study.

Drysdale switched on the lights, illuminating a very
functional, very masculine room in complete contrast to
the rest of the house. Gracious like his wife, Drysdale
stayed on for a moment to ask more of Athol McFarlane's
health then he excused himself saying he had better get
back to his guests. Luke took an armchair, upholstered in
a rich dark green leather, allowing his eyes to wander casually around the room, his mind preoccupied with this
coming meeting. Four long months since he'd seen Storm.
It felt like years. Sick of her, sick with her. Hell it was
like a disease!

He heard the tap of her high heels along the corridor,
an excitement in itself as he forcefully inhaled a lungful
of breath. She was there! Sweeping into the room in a
cloud of some beautiful elusive perfume that made him
flare his nostrils, a subtle blend of gardenia, orange blos-
som, freesia? What would a man know? What would a
mere male know about the miracle of Woman? She be-
dazzled him in her sexy little sequined top in lime-green
with a long side split ruffled skirt that had to be chiffon
over silk, the tiny green iridescent beads that were sewn
all over it catching the light. Her thick raven tresses were
dressed more elaborately than he had yet seen, the volume
increased so it winged back from her forehead and cheeks
and spilt over her bare shoulders. Knowing her so well, he

could see she had gone pale, her green eyes glittering like the emeralds she wore in her ears.

So near, yet so far! She made his head reel and she was using up his life.

"Luke, what is it? What's the matter?" she asked urgently, closing the study door behind her and leaning back against it.

It was quite a pose, a sizzler, but he knew it was unconscious. "Hi there, Storm," he said, getting slowly to his feet. "I'm really happy to see you, too. No need to panic. Your father sent me."

She could hardly speak for her surprise. Luke, as handsome, as inflammable as ever. "About what? Has he taken ill?" Though her heart quickened with fright, it came out like a challenge.

"You mean you didn't know?" he clipped off, his mood darkening. "Your father has been ill for years."

She couldn't bear the censure in his beautiful blue eyes. "I only spoke to him last night. He was perfectly all right then."

He could feel the familiar tension invading his body. "Don't be absurd, Storm. His leg gives him hell as you know."

That had its effect, too. "What are you accusing me of, Luke?" she asked heatedly, wondering if their clashes were to be repeated forever.

"Well, now we're on the subject, I'm accusing you of neglect."

She flushed, the upsurge of colour increasing her beauty. "Don't you always pick the right words," she said bleakly. "I love my father. I ring him regularly."

"But you don't visit."

She shook back her long hair. The overhead light had burnished the ebony waves with purple. "I have a *career,*

Luke. Can't you understand? I have commissions I must complete. And I get them from people with the money to afford them. Like the people who are here tonight. I just can't rush off at a moment's notice."

He looked at her unsmilingly. "Well you're going to have to. Your father wants you home. I think you should come."

She laughed. It was almost certainly not humorous. "*You* think…*you* think. Oh, yes, you decide what's best."

"Don't start," he begged. "I've had just about enough. You know and I know that you stay away because of me."

"How you kid yourself!" The truth didn't lessen the pain.

"I don't. You can't put anything over me. I'm not your father to be wound around your little finger. Busy or not I want you to come back with me. You have the wedding tomorrow, but Sunday."

She stared at him, absorbing the aura of power that surrounded him. "You can't be serious?"

"I'm always serious with you. Your father wants you."

Anxiety was like a knife against her heart but she knew her father. He thought bringing her home was his right. Twenty-seven and he still treated her like a child. "It can't be that serious, Luke. He would have told me."

"Are you sure of that?"

"So you're calling the shots now?" She was as defensive as ever. There was so much bottled up inside her it might never get out.

"I always act in the interests of your father. It's over four months since you've seen him. I have to tell you he's gone downhill since then."

"Oh God!" She all but swayed into a chair, the slit in her long skirt revealing one long, slender leg. "I ring him every week without fail. Why does he never *say* anything? Why is everything so secret?"

"You know your father," Luke sighed. "He plays it close to the chest. Besides the last thing he wants to do is cause you anxiety."

"And what about you?" There was the pain again. Not jealousy. Rejection. "You're always there aren't you? He has you to confide in."

"Well he doesn't," Luke responded curtly, all the feeling he had about her cruelly twisting. "I tried to speak to Tom Skinner but Tom clams up."

"Do you really think I haven't tried to speak to Tom myself?" Storm flung up her head. "Tom does what Dad tells him. Just like everyone else. Including *you.*"

"And you of course are the rebel?" He let his blue eyes wander over her body, so beautiful and so insufferable. "I'm sorry if it interferes with your professional and social life but I feel you should come home if only for a few days."

"Is that an order?"

"It's a request. Don't close your heart, Storm."

"Then it's that bad?" Her almond eyes glittered with unshed tears.

"I wouldn't be here otherwise. We're never going to be friends, Storm, but I do care about your father," he said, fighting down the mad desire to crush her in his arms.

"And he *loves* you." She had been exposed to that early. "What is it about you men that you value your sons above your daughters?"

"I don't accept that," he said, thinking to have a little daughter like Storm would be utter joy.

"It's true in Dad's case. I spent years of my childhood wishing I were a boy. Wishing I were you." She shook her head. She had been wounded in so many ways perhaps no one would understand.

The pathos of that stung him. "I'm sorry, Storm. I never asked for any of it."

"Of course not." Her smile was bitter-sweet. "It was your destiny. What are you really after, Luke. We both know you're ambitious. Is it Winding River? I swear you'll never get it." Her feelings for him, so complex, manifested themselves in inflicting hurt.

His eyes flashed. "If anything happens to your father, Storm, I'm *out*. Nothing on God's earth would persuade me to work for you. And you couldn't run the station yourself. You've taken no interest in it for years."

"Who needed my interest?" she said, in reality a victim of her father's blind injustice. "Who needs me when they've got you?"

"God, Storm, I'm not a monster," he rasped. "I'm no substitute for you when it comes to your father. He *idolizes* you, but you've always been too hot-headed to accept that. So he's one of the old school who thinks women have to be protected and provided for; shielded from the harsh realities of life. I understand perfectly how important your career is to you. I applaud you. But your father has given you everything you've got including your apartment."

That he knew was a double blow. "You know that?" she asked.

"You just told me." He moved restlessly, rangy and powerful. "How could you have afforded it anyway? It's only these last few years you've been making real money. I expect that your father makes you a handsome allowance. That dress must have cost a fortune." It was exquisite revealing her beautiful shoulders and the swell of her breasts. "The sandals. The emeralds in your ears."

"My mother's emeralds, Luke," she pointed out dryly.

"Columbian. Real emeralds are very hard to come by. You don't know everything."

He drew a deep steadying breath. "Look, why don't we put our little range war aside. I didn't come here for *you* I came for your father. Because I care about him. Like you he's given me just about everything but I work very hard to repay him. In fact I break my back."

"It's just like I said, Luke," she continued with the right mix of irony and humour. "You're hero material. The son Dad always wanted."

"And therein lies a lifetime of grief."

"I don't think it would be excessive to say you stole my birthright."

"That cuts deep. You know I didn't steal anything," he retorted with some passion. "Chance affected our lives."

"It certainly put paid to any civilised relationship between us," she said, hiding her sick regrets. "I used to think when I was just a girl the two of you deliberately tried to exclude me."

As a man he could understand that. "Now you know better." His expression gentled.

"Maybe I can't see the light even yet." Abruptly her tone changed. "Did you fly Dad's Cessna?"

He responded curtly to the near taunt. "The quickest way to get here."

"When do you intend flying back?"

"As soon as you're packed."

She searched the eyes that blazed out of his tanned skin. "You truly think it's that urgent? Dad likes to keep hold of us both. He says he's proud of my success but he'd have been far happier if I'd stayed at home dancing attendance on him. No, don't shrug it off, Luke. *Listen.* 'You're an heiress. You don't have to work!' What he really meant was he wants me to be financially and emotionally dependant on him. I'm not such a fool I don't know my own father. He's an important man, much respected, everyone speaks of him with such admiration—the way he reared me single-handedly.

"I've had a lot of time to think about it. Dad is first and foremost the big man in a man's world. He's lived like that all his life. Athol McFarlane, the cattle baron. The Major. A man among men. He's always said he never married because of his grief. He could have had any woman he wanted. He didn't have to marry a one of them, and you know there were a few. Dad didn't really want to remarry. He might have been having second thoughts about a son but you came along. Ready-made. To make the grand plan complete, you lost your parents."

He thrust a hand through his hair, the light above him capturing its dark fire. "I don't appreciate your talking about my parents."

"Why not?" she flared. "You talk all the time about mine. Anyway I was close to them, Luke. Don't forget that. Your mother used to call me Princess even if it was a joke."

"It was no joke," he told her. "You gave her joy."

Storm's green eyes turned deeply reflective. "Some people might think my father was rather cruel. Maybe unknowingly, he's not the most sensitive of men, but he never for one minute sees a woman as an equal."

It was perfectly true. Women to the Major were ornaments to be worn on a man's arm. "That might be, Storm," he agreed, saddened all at once. "But in his own way he loves you dearly."

She pressed back in the armchair. "That love has been a bit destructive, wouldn't you say? I'm also thinking this could be just a stunt to get me home. Since he's been so inactive Dad sits around making plans. Much as I love him I know he manipulates us both.''

"Agreed. I'm no fool, either." The muscles along his chiselled jaw bunched. "I can only give you my spin on this. Your father is genuinely ill. Noni agrees with me. God, Storm, I didn't fly all the way here for a psychological analysis, informed as it may be. You're bitter and you feel betrayed. Maybe your father *is* ruthless but in the most benign way.''

"As though there's any such thing." She half smiled, a poignant movement of her lovely full mouth.

He had to look away. "If you love your father as much as you say, you'll come. No one is asking you to bury yourself in the wilds. A few days. Hell, can't you spare him that?" An image of the Major's gaunt face filled his mind.

Storm winced at the implication she was pitiless. In truth she felt defeated. Defeated by her love for her father, defeated by the messed up feelings she had for Luke. It seemed to her she had fought the both of them for most of her life.

"All right, you both win." She rose in one graceful movement, holding his eyes. Eyes that had haunted her every move. "It won't be easy but I'll be ready on Sunday. Does that suit?"

"That will be fine," he said. "You won't regret it." He was struggling not to stare at her, but the compulsion to do so was too strong for him. Her green almond eyes were so brilliant they might have had tears in them. "I should go," he said, keeping a safe distance from her with the pure force of his will.

"Actually Stephanie is determined you stay. You could be the toast of the evening if you wanted to."

"Don't be so ridiculous," he answered shortly, hostility flickering back and forth between them.

"That's a good thing about you, Luke. You have no vanity."

"Go on, anything else?" She had begun to walk to the door, now he followed her up.

"Surely Carla tells you how wonderful you are?" She swept about unexpectedly the sarcastic comment dying on her lips when she found him so close. Their bodies were only inches apart. Taller than average, Storm always felt at such a disadvantage with Luke towering over her. The physical shock of those blue, blue, eyes. That rich red hair! My God! It was like a detonator going off. Her heart quickened and she felt this great surge of what could only be excitement. This was a *man*. She felt his sexuality in every cell of her body.

"I wonder what would happen if we were cast up together on a desert island?" He gave her a mere shadow of his illuminating smile. Yet it drugged her. "No Major. No Winding River?"

"No past," she added as her defence mechanism kicked in. "We can't escape it."

His expression that had created such an erotic disturbance in her changed. "I'll go." Their relationship had not developed as other relationships did. He would be a fool to think anything could change. "Would you thank Mrs. Drysdale for her kind invitation but explain now you're coming back with me I have more things to attend to."

Incredibly she felt keen disappointment. "Don't let me put you off. Sara may be getting married tomorrow but I think she's reliving the intoxication of her holidays on the station. And you didn't even kiss her. Or *did* you?"

He dipped his dark red head. "I have to say I don't remember. There are so many girls I've kissed."

"I know," she answered. "You're notorious for getting women to fall in love with you."

They were making their way down the corridor when a tall, well-built young man with floppy blond hair dressed in immaculate dinner clothes, trailing Sara in his wake, approached. "Storm darling! I'd been looking for you everywhere until Sara told me you were trapped in the study."

"I did *not!*" Sara didn't hesitate to say indignantly.

"Good grief isn't that Alex, the ex-fiancé?" Luke murmured, lowering his head to be close to Storm's ear. "Pain in the neck, as ever."

The ex-fiancé had recognised Luke, too. "Well for goodness' sake!" he cried, without enthusiasm, "if it isn't..." He pretended to think for a moment. "Luke?"

As though he didn't know. Storm had brought him to the station several times during their year-long engagement. Luke nodded amiably. "I've been called that all my life. How's it going, Alex?"

"Great! Just great." Alex and Sara drew closer. "I thought Sara might be pulling my leg when she said you were here."

"Surprise visit." Luke offered laconically.

"Oh, what for?" Alex zeroed right in, his expression challenging but a mite troubled.

"Family matters, Alex," Storm said in a cool voice. "It's not Luke's job to explain."

"No, no, of course not," Alex smiled at her backing off. "Nice to say hello to you, Luke. I expect you're off now, message delivered?"

"As a matter of fact he's staying!" Sara tripped over to Luke and clung to his arm. "Stephanie took quite a fancy to him. On sight."

"This guy is clever!" Alex feigned admiration, at the same time noticing Branagan looked extraordinarily good. "I have to say he does bring in a whiff of the great outdoors." He gave a condescending smile.

"Well now you know what a cattleman looks like." Sara smiled brightly. "Pretty terrific, I'd say. Everyone seems impressed. Except, maybe you, Alex," she added, taking a shot at him.

"Not at all. You misunderstand me," Alex dropped his languid tone, moving toward Storm and taking her hand. "Storm, dearest, can't I carry you off? Everyone's missing you."

"Oh, I don't think so," she gave a little laugh, gently withdrawing her hand. "I must see Luke to the door. We have a few things to finalise."

"You're not going surely?" Sara looked up at Luke's handsome profile, her sweet expression registering acute disappointment.

"You heard the lady," Luke mocked, glancing towards Storm. "I'm being shown the door."

"Of course you aren't." Storm shook her head.

"No, actually, Sara, I do have things to attend to, but it's been great seeing you." Luke bent to kiss her cheek. "Every good wish for tomorrow. You're going to make a beautiful bride."

"Yes, I am!" Sara beamed. "Why don't you come along? You're here not a thousand miles away. We can always fit in one more friend of the bride. It would be lovely wouldn't it, Storm?" She glanced at her friend. "You should see the dresses. They're gorgeous. Storm, as my dearest girlfriend is chief bridesmaid. She's wearing a beautiful gold matt satin and guipure lace gown. She'll look out of this world."

Luke nodded. "She's got a talent for doing that. Don't

worry. I'll see it in the papers and magazines. It doesn't take all that long for them to reach us. Thank you for the thought, Sara, but I must decline. There are errands to run for the Major.'' True enough but the thought of seeing Storm in her bridesmaid's finery was more than he could bear.

"How *is* the Major?'' Alex asked belatedly. This when he'd been shown lavish hospitality on his visits.

"Not as well as we want,'' Luke said, then sketched an attractive little salute, more to Sara than Alex. "I'll say good night. Enjoy yourselves.''

"Hurry back, Storm,'' Alex pleaded.

"Bye, bye, Luke,'' Sara called as he moved away with Storm at his shoulder.

"You'll make my excuses to Mr. and Mrs. Drysdale, won't you?'' Luke double-checked as they arrived at the front door. Guests crossing from one splendid reception room to the other glanced at them with bright curiosity but Storm didn't appear to notice.

She indicated they step outside, the night breeze lifting her hair and wafting her perfume to him, an alluring intoxicant. "Of course,'' she promised, then as an afterthought. "How are you getting back into town?''

"I thought you'd never ask,'' he mocked, gazing back at her while he moved down a step. "Same way I got here. By cab. I've got my mobile or I might just keep walking. It's a beautiful night and it's not that far.''

"Too far for most people,'' she smiled, thinking how they both had been raised. Alex fit as he was, would never have considered it. "What time Sunday?''

He shrugged his wide shoulders that tapered to a narrow waist, expelling sex appeal in every pore. "I'd like to make it early but I doubt if you'll be ready for an early-morning start. Not after the wedding.''

She responded from long habit as if she'd been challenged. "You think I'm going to get drunk?"

"No more than usual, but I think you'll be tired. It's a late-afternoon wedding. The reception will go on for hours. Is the ex invited?"

"What do you think?" Paradoxically she wanted to reach out and touch him. The night around them was playing tricks.

"It sounds as though it might be on again." He launched into an excellent imitation of Alex's well-bred languid tones. "Storm, darling! I've been looking for you everywhere."

"You always did have a gift for mimicry. Remember when you—" She broke off. "It isn't on again with Alex. Not that it's any of your business."

"No more than your inquiry about Carla," he returned directly. "We have to stop off briefly at Mingari by the way. I have some freight to unload."

"Sure it's not just an excuse to see Carla?" She shot him a glance; the greenest flame. "How is she anyway?"

"You'll be able to see for yourself," he returned mildly. "She always asks after you."

She smiled without humour. "Do you know I think that has something to do with you? So what time in the morning?" She didn't look at him but stared over his head at the starlit night.

He took the rest of the steps with two easy strides, looking back at her, her lovely figure silhouetted against the light from the great chandelier in the entrance hall. Such a complicated existence he led. This was one woman denied him. "I'll be outside your apartment block at eight o'clock and that's a concession," he said more crisply than he intended.

"You really believe I still can't get up at dawn?"

"A rhetorical question, Miss McFarlane." He bowed. "Let me say instead I believe you can do anything you set your mind to. Not that it always works. To put it bluntly you've made as many mistakes as I have. Good night. Enjoy the big day tomorrow."

"I will." She remained still where she was watching him stride down the drive. Where Luke was concerned she was very, very vulnerable. It was something she had known all her life.

CHAPTER THREE

SHE was ready waiting for him at the front of her apartment building when he arrived in a hired car he must have organised the day before.

"All set?" He was out of the car moving towards her, perpetually virile, vivid, dynamic. She had to concede a glamorous figure with that superb lean body that made the most casual clothes look great.

"Two pieces of luggage," she said, colourful enough herself in a violet silk shirt tucked into skinny black trousers, high black boots, an Armani leather jacket draped around her shoulders. It was late winter in Sydney but it would be a lot hotter where she was going; except at night when the desert gave up its heat and the temperatures dropped dramatically.

Both looked and sounded brisk. A feat for Storm because she had quite a headache from the wedding. It had gone off so wonderfully well it had turned into a bit of a circus towards the end. She told Luke this in answer to his questions while he loaded her expensive luggage into the boot, then she slipped into the front passenger seat, trying to disengage herself from all physical sensation. Luke's aura was so powerful it scarcely let her breathe. In fact she reasoned she had spent most of her life fighting to get out of the shadow of the two most influential men in her life. Her father and Luke. God knows what she thought she had been doing getting herself engaged; first to Patrick, some ten years older and a very successful lawyer, then to Alex, more her own age who worked for his father in a leading stock broking firm. Alex couldn't fight out from under his father's shadow, either. She didn't think he ever would, but she was doing all right. Her name was a current buzzword since she was a finalist in the De Beers Diamonds International Award. It had been won by a fellow Australian—a brilliant young man with his amazing diamond mask. Not bad for more than 25000 entrants worldwide. Her father had told her he was thrilled for her when she rang to tell him the exciting news. Her piece, an elaborate creation for the hair, when elaborate jewellery was the fashion, her father, strangely enough had never asked to see it. She had heard much later that Luke had told her father it was an "incredible honour and he would have loved to travel to see the piece." He never had. A pity!

"What in the world's wrong with you?" Luke asked eventually as they approached the freeway. It was fairly early on Sunday morning and things were blissfully quiet. No crowds, no traffic jams to contend with.

"Lost in my thoughts." She glanced at him for a fraction of a second, not wanting him to intrude too much on them.

"You're not interested in conversation?"

"I thought you had me under heavy fire, Luke."

"Not at all." He shook his head. "I just want you to see your father face-to-face. I want you to give me the benefit of your opinion. I also want you to give him the comfort only *you* can bring."

"You should have been a politician," she said dryly.

"I've never wanted to be anything else but a cattleman like my dad. One of these days when I'm no longer needed on Winding River I'm going to start my own operation."

"Are you really?" she asked somewhat cynically when she knew perfectly well Luke was indispensable on

Winding River. Highly intelligent, well educated, Luke at twenty-nine was no pale substitute for her father. He was an extremely astute businessman, which he had to be these days in a fiercely competitive market. As well he was a consummate cattleman, and a born communicator. Luke was Luke. Dammit, Luke was unique.

"It's my dream to run my own show." Luke was almost talking to himself. "The Major and I see practically eye-to-eye on most issues, but occasionally I would have preferred to back my own judgement."

"Good grief, a criticism of Dad." She gave a little laugh, flinging her glossy hair over her shoulder.

"Think about it, Storm," he urged. "Don't I always say what I think, but you have to remember the Major has been too good to me to ever forget it."

Couldn't Luke *see* her father, in lavishing so much attention on him, had taken it from her? Storm sighed and gazed down at her ringless hands. She could have Alex's ring back anytime she wanted. "The thing is, Luke, Dad knew what he was doing. You always had that marvellous potential. That quality that sets men apart. You don't think Dad missed it. He always had you lined up for a top job. He thinks ahead. He has to after all, but he manipulates people. He manipulates lives. I'm not trying to make him out any sort of a monster or exorcise my own personal devils but I wouldn't need to be a genius to work Dad out."

He frowned as though the Major could do no wrong. "Since you're being so candid, could I say sometimes you sound like you hate your own father?"

"You're out of your brain," she said wearily, her equilibrium destroyed. Wasn't that the reason she stayed away?

"Am I?" Luke asked ironically. "There's a whole lot of angst there."

"I have to agree with you," she said sweetly. "Put it down to the way I was raised." Storm put her head back against the headrest and closed her eyes. She was a woman of intuition after all. She knew in her bones, even if Luke, blinded by devotion to her father, didn't, the Major was planning something that would involve them both. Whatever it was they would be expected to obey.

After hours in the air they finally landed on Mingari Station's airstrip, Luke making a perfect touch down despite the strong cross-winds. He was as good a pilot as he was everything else, she thought, yielding to admiration. Magnetic to women. All of her women friends had noted his brief appearance at the Drysdale party, professing their amazement some lucky woman hadn't snaffled him up. A lot had tried, she'd replied. Storm had her pilot's licence, too, but she hadn't been keeping up with her weekend flying times as much as she should have been. She's been too darn busy. The Mingari hangar was coming up.

My country! She thought as she gazed out the window. This infinite red land shimmering beneath the blazing blue vault of the sky. The liberating feel of it! The scent of the bush, the sunlit trees, the sight of horses and stockmen, working dogs, great herds of cattle. This was where her heart was and she had been driven away. It was like a great weight on her heart the way her father had cut her out of what she always thought of as her heritage. He had excluded her from all station business. He'd never discussed with her anything pertaining to the McFarlane operations, which were big. Women weren't supposed to bother their pretty little heads with such things. A woman's job was to look after her man. Have the babies. Run the homesteads. There a woman could reign supreme. She could be as active as she liked in women's affairs, but she shouldn't aspire to learning the business.

For years she had tried, bewildered by her father's attitude in this day and age. She had a good brain—she had to accept there were a few limitations attached to her sex— but letting her into the charmed circle, the men's club, would have made life tolerable. Why were heirs much more valued than heiresses? she agonized. She couldn't understand it. For years it had made her singularly unhappy. Sometimes when she faced the naked truth she saw clearly that Luke had always treated her as an equal. Maybe even put her up on pedestal. Instead of being a comfort, it had made her resent him. Other feelings she had for him were so subterranean she had even managed to keep them from herself.

Carla, who had never been under such restraints, was waiting for them near the hangar, waving, smiling, almost dancing up and down in her excitement. No sign of her father, Phillip Prentice, a close friend of the Major's. Carla, unlike Storm, was very much a part of the Prentice organization although Carla had two older brothers who worked with their father to run the huge station. Mingari was Winding River's nearest neighbour on the northwest border. This was the Channel Country, fabled area of the giant cattle kingdoms irrigated by the countless maze of waterways that ran into the Diamantina, Georgina, the Barcoo and Cooper's Creek. Rivers that flowed towards the greatest salt lake in the world, Lake Eyre, Mowana Mowana to the aboriginals. Mowana Mowana rarely filled, perhaps a few times in a century. But when it did! The sight was even more miraculous than the coming of the wildflowers after rains.

"Storm, how wonderful to see you!" Carla rushed forward to greet her, a tall athletic young woman with short dark curly hair, lovely golden-brown eyes, clear golden skin and a shapely figure. The whole thing added up to a very attractive package indeed. "You've got *thin!*"

"Do you think so?" Both of them kissed air. Storm knew from way back Carla had never been one of her fans. Of course it all had to do with Luke. How ironic! "I was a bridesmaid yesterday. I had to make sure I was able to fit into the dress." In fact she maintained her light weight and still managed to eat sensibly.

Luke, too, scored a kiss. This time not the air but right on his clean-cut mouth, Carla's lips parted and clinging. She found she couldn't look to see how Luke was reacting. In fact the sight for some inexplicable reason came like a tremendous shock. It served to remind her just how complicated her relationship with Luke was.

Carla drew back, her golden-brown eyes dancing. She linked her arm through Luke's. "Let's go back to the house and have lunch. I bet you're starving."

Storm answered quickly, too quickly. "That would be lovely, Carla, but Dad will be expecting us."

"He won't begrudge us *an hour,* surely?" Carla asked with high good humour not relinquishing her hold on Luke. "Besides Mum and I have everything prepared. Just cold meats and salad. Nothing fancy. Dad and the boys are coming in. They just love to see Luke. And they'll be thrilled to see you, too, Storm. Jason has never forgiven you for getting engaged to someone else."

As though she'd ever looked sideways at Jason Prentice.

"All right, Storm?" Luke's eyes held hers a moment, allowing her to make the decision.

She couldn't be anything else but gracious. "Fine, Carla, you've gone to so much trouble. It will be nice to see the family again, but I wouldn't like to delay too long.

I've been so busy lately my visits home have become precious.''

"Wonderful, then that's settled!" Carla turned a sparkling face to Luke's. "You've left me on my lonesome too long," she said decidedly provocatively. "Amy and Wes Richards are all set up to give a big party in a fortnight's time. Coming along?"

"Well I've been invited." Luke smiled. "I'll be trying to make it. It all depends what goes on back home."

Home!

It was said so simply, Storm thought. Luke had staked his claim.

Mingari homestead, though it couldn't vie with the grandness of Winding River's homestead, nevertheless had its own charm. A large colonial-style building painted white with dark green shutters and a green corrugated iron roof, had been added to over the decades so that it rambled over a considerable area. Station horses grazed in a paddock nearby, and a kangaroo with a joey in its pouch hopped leisurely away into the lightly timbered grounds dotted with flowering bauhinias, as they swept up the drive.

Karen Prentice was waiting for them on the wide verandah, still so slim and attractive she looked more like Carla's sister than her mother. Both women had their sights firmly set on Luke. Carla in hopes of a husband. Karen doing her best to help her daughter. Neither of them was about to give up and it wasn't as though they hadn't been trying hard. Storm on the other hand was just a mite tricky; the Major's only daughter but not a great favourite. Storm had gained the impression for reasons of their own both women considered she offered some threat to their plans. At any rate courtesy prevailed, even if the smiles wore a bit thin.

Clive Prentice and his fine-looking sons, Jason and Daniel duly arrived and the greetings began all over again. The conversation sparkled with camaraderie, the men shaking hands; Luke came in for some back-slapping. Storm thereafter became the object of Jason's exclusive attentions, which she found idiotic. Eventually they went into lunch served on the very pleasant plant-filled rear patio. More lavish than Carla had suggested, there were platters of thickly sliced ham, turkey and cold roast beef accompanied by two superb salads, one Greek, one Thai, a creamy red and white cabbage coleslaw, the Prentice men particularly liked, with plenty of warm crusty loaves fresh from the oven flavoured with goat's cheese, potato and rosemary. White wine was offered; the men drank a couple of cold beers, no more. There was work to be done. Storm declined the wine, her head was aching enough.

"Why you've scarcely eaten a thing!" Carla waited her moment to call attention to Storm's half-eaten plate, as though it offered clear evidence of anorexia.

"What I had was delicious, thank you." Storm set down her knife and fork. "You must forgive me but I have a headache."

"I expect you got up incredibly early," Carla said, her attractive face a picture of sympathy.

"I can't remember a time when I didn't," Storm laughed. "The wedding I attended went on into the small hours. I stayed until after one. I had to. I was the chief bridesmaid."

"I bet you looked absolutely beautiful," Jason drooled, the expression on his face suggesting he was visualizing the scene.

"The bride looked better," Storm replied. Sara really had looked radiant.

Although it appeared very much like the family was

hoping they'd stay longer, it was Luke who came to Storm's rescue, gently refusing coffee. "Many thanks for your hospitality." He swept them all with his marvellous white smile. "That was a great pick-me-up but we mustn't keep the Major waiting any longer."

"I'll drive you back to the plane," Carla offered, springing up to hold his hand.

"By the way, Luke." Clive Prentice, a good-looking heavy-set man stood up. "I've been racking my brain to try and remember that Argentinean rancher's name. The guy the Major invited out about eighteen months ago. A great polo player."

"Otero," Luke replied. "Richard Otero. A really nice guy. What made you think of him?"

Storm didn't catch the answer. Karen Prentice returned from the house with a couple of painkillers and a glass of water. "Here, Storm, swallow these down," she urged. "You should have told me at the outset about your headache, my dear."

"It's not all that bad." Storm took the tablets gratefully. "Thank you, Karen."

Karen nodded, waiting while Storm swallowed the tablets. "Tell me, dear, how long are you staying this time?" she asked, just barely disguising the fact she hoped it wouldn't be more than a week.

"That depends on how Dad is. He keeps such a lot to himself but Luke thought I should come home."

Karen raised her nicely marked brows. "He flew all the way into Sydney for you?"

"Dad's plane, Karen. Dad wanted him to."

"Of course," Karen backed off. "We're all so proud of you. You always were such a gifted girl when Carla hated boarding school. I know the Major misses you dreadfully but I'm sure he realises you *must* live in Sydney for your work.''

''Actually I could work anywhere,'' Storm said, prompted into a touch of perversity, ''and sell through a gallery or certain jewellers. A lot of my work these days is commissions.''

''You mean you might consider coming home for good?'' Karen looked pained then mustered a smile.

''As I said, Karen, that all depends on Dad,'' Storm reminded her gently.

Why did Carla and her mother have such trouble understanding she had no designs on Luke nor he on her? They were quite incompatible.

When they landed on Winding River she was surprised and touched to see quite a few of the station staff had turned out to greet her. Stockmen, some of whom she had known all of her life, the new jackeroos, station wives with little children, friends from the aboriginal community. Storm walked down the line shaking everyone's hand and bestowing a kiss on each and every child. One new baby had arrived in her absence but she was glad she had remembered to send a card and some useful things for the layette. It was such a delight buying for a baby that she had gone a touch overboard but the young mother, Kalle, now thanked her gratefully holding up her adorable child for Storm's sweet kiss. These were the moments Storm found so rewarding. The knowledge that people on the station really cared about her and loved to see her home. The thought exhilarated her and set her free of her slight depression. The headache had disappeared as well.

When she and Luke walked up onto the verandah of the homestead, Noni rushed out, her arms outstretched. ''Hello, hello, hello, darling girl!''

"Noni!" She embraced the woman who had been her support during many a fractious time.

"Your dad is waiting for you in the conservatory," Noni said happily. "He's a bit emotional with all the excitement. Hi there, Luke." Noni beamed, looking past Storm to the striking young man lounging back against a pillar quietly watching. Elegant and full of energy. That was Luke. It was quite a combination.

"Hi, Noni." He returned the smile lazily. "We stopped off at Mingari—I had some freight to unload. Karen invited us to lunch."

"Nice of her and so difficult to get out of," Storm supplied. "I hope Dad wasn't getting impatient?"

"Just a bit!" Noni admitted, studying Storm with pleasure. Everything ran very smoothly as long as everything fitted into the Major's schedule. "So you won't want a cup of tea?"

"I never say no to a cup of tea, Noni," Storm laughed. "Still black with a slice of lemon."

"Well I must go." Luke uncrossed his arms, preparatory to moving off. "There's always something that needs attention." He stood on the top step.

Noni drew a hasty breath. "I think the Major is expecting you, too, Luke," she said, thinking the Major could have received Storm on her own. Just this once.

"Another time, Noni," Luke said with a faint note of wonderment. "I'm sure he'll want to see Storm on her own."

"Not true." Storm's green eyes swept him ironically. "Why should this visit be different to any others? You'd better come, Luke. We both toe the line."

"If that's what it is," he replied, his chiselled mouth tight. "Please tell the Major I need to catch up."

"Of course," Storm answered smoothly. It was wrong

of her but she couldn't stop. "When its all's said and done Dad is really at *your* mercy."

"Storm, love." Noni tried to intervene, taking a few small steps to come between them.

It lessened the tension a shade. "So long!" Luke's handsome features were taut as he walked off.

"That didn't help, love." Noni turned back at this beautiful, beautiful girl who often tore her heart out. "Luke is such a good man."

A bitter-sweet smile played around Storm's lovely mouth. "He's everything a man should be. Not sarcasm. *Really,*" she answered without a trace of humour. "Give me a minute to freshen up then I'll come down. How is Dad today?" She took Noni's arm as they walked into the entrance hall. "Luke told me you're both worried about him."

Noni sighed. "I'd say he's in constant pain now but he never talks about it, never complains. You're going to be the best medicine any doctor could order up."

Storm gave the housekeeper a little hug, a glint in her eye. "You flatter me, Noni," she said. "Dad had *two* children. Didn't you know that?"

Athol McFarlane stood up the minute his daughter entered the room. "Storm, darling," he said, his expression so charged with feeling it was fierce.

"Daddy!" Storm went to him, her green eyes filling with tears of sadness and guilt. Only four months yet her father seemed to have aged ten years. Not the work of time. The work of pain. The piercing grey eyes looked sunken and bruised, harsh lines were etched into his tanned skin, his once powerful frame gaunt and thin.

"It's so good to have you home." He hugged her as

though he never wanted to let her go. Something that opened Storm's heart until he said, "Where's Luke?"

Storm drew back, trying to recover her emotional balance. "He's gone back to work. He's concerned about losing time. He likes to keep on top of things."

"I wanted him to be here." McFarlane frowned, obviously put out.

"Aren't I enough, Dad?" she asked quietly, smiling a little.

"Storm!" It was a cry from the heart even as he refused to see he had created a wall between them. "You're more than enough, but I thought Luke should join us. Sit down, darling. Tell me what you've been doing?" He winced as he resumed his seat in a high-backed leather armchair with a rest for his feet.

"Perhaps you'd better tell me what you've been doing first?" Storm drew her chair closer to him. "You don't look well, Dad." A serious understatement but knowing her father she couldn't overstate it. "What does the doctor have to say?"

Her father didn't rise to that. "The same old thing. I'm wearing out. The leg gives me gip from time to time."

"Perhaps I should speak to Tom myself?" She didn't say she already had. Several times. "Would you mind?"

Her father's mouth compressed. "It's the worst possible thing you could do. I'll keep you informed."

"But you wanted me home, Dad," Storm persisted gently. "That must mean something?"

His dark bushy eyebrows drew together. "I don't think it's so unusual for a man to want to see his only daughter surely?"

"Only *child*."

He didn't attempt to study her meaning. "I've told you many times, Storm, I'd build you a studio. Outfit it with everything you want. Convert rooms in the house if you like. I don't expect you to stay with me all the time. You could fly off any time you liked for a week or so. Take a break. See your friends. Have a good time. I need you here, Storm. It's as simple as that."

There was a tremor in his stern voice now that further upset her. "Something is wrong, Dad. Why won't you confide in me?"

"Would it make any difference if I did?" he asked abruptly, brushing at his nose as if at an irritant.

"It would make a big difference," Storm said, succeeding in preventing her own voice turning cold. "I love you, Dad."

"You say it as though I doubted it," McFarlane calmed down, folding his large hands in front of him, his expression turning pensive. "But if you love me, Storm, you wouldn't go away."

Slowly she shook her dark head. "Don't do this, Dad," she begged quietly. "I have a career. I'm a success. I have a life."

"Your life is here!" Suddenly anger flared.

"I don't see it that way, Dad." Storm had never been one to be intimidated. She wasn't now but she was shaken by her father's appearance. "Please don't let's argue. I've only just arrived home."

But his anger hadn't completely vanished. "How long do you propose to stay?"

"As long as I can."

Her father moved restlessly, his shoulders slumped. "Where did you say Luke was?"

The headache that had disappeared began to throb. "What has Luke got to do with this, Dad?" Her voice gentled in entreaty. "I'm your own flesh and blood."

"Now that sounds familiar." McFarlane raised his head

to give her a half amused, half impatient look. "Dammit, girl, I've never understood why you're so jealous of Luke."

Storm rubbed her temples. "I have no defence, Dad. I just *am*."

"But that's just plain perverse," McFarlane burst out. "He's such a splendid young man," he continued, looking puzzled. "You two should have been the closest friends. I've seen the young men you've invited here over the years. The fiancés. God they couldn't hold a candle to Luke," he said with open contempt.

She tried not to bridle. It was pointless anyway. "But then I was in love with them, Dad. Or I thought I was."

His answer was a wry snort. "I can't tell you how relieved I was when you finally came to your senses. It's time you got married, Storm. But to the *right* man."

"Who is?" Her gaze was direct and challenging. No wonder people whispered, she thought. No wonder Carla looked at her with suspicion.

McFarlane brushed a hand across his thick thatch of hair, a temporising gesture. "A man you can give your whole heart to," he offered. "A man you can respect and admire. A strong man, Storm," he added with humour. "One who can keep you in line."

"You think women need keeping in line?" She gave him a little, crooked smile.

"By and large they do. Especially you. You've always fought the least suggestion of authority."

She felt a twinge of guilt. "So I did. But I'm not here to fight you, Dad. I'm here to offer comfort." She leaned forward and took her father's hand. "It's like I said. I love you."

"I love you, too, darling." He stopped abruptly. There were tears in his eyes.

Tears from her father! It shocked Storm so much she jumped up and hugged him, letting her cheek rest against the top of his head. "Dad, Dad," she crooned.

Her father patted her hand, his voice soft and unless she was paranoid, a shade triumphant. "Make sure Luke knows to come up to dinner," he said. "It will be wonderful, the three of us together."

Falls the shadow.

There was sadness in her eyes but Storm made a supreme effort to answer cheerfully. "Sure, Dad. I'd like to go for a ride this afternoon. I'll tell him then."

Noni arrived with the tea, freshly baked cookies and some little almond tarts, well pleased when Storm and the Major asked her to sit down and join them.

The atmosphere immediately lightened. Noni had that enviable effect on people, Storm thought. She sat back, beginning to entertain them both with an account of the wedding; her most recent showing; her sales to a couple of very-much-in-the-news society women, plus a wealth of light, amusing gossip. She wished it were always so simple to make her father laugh.

Late afternoon while her father was taking a nap: "Just like a child!" he said. "I actually need it." Storm took out one of her favourite horses, Rising Star, an ex-racehorse whose delight in galloping Storm found exhilarating. A good gallop would clear the cobwebs. She loved horses. Loved riding. She'd felt confident and comfortable on a horse's back. She had done ever since she could remember.

There were photographs of her up in the saddle at age three, hard hat on her head, little striped polo shirt, jodhpurs, shiny boots on her feet. Photographs of her on horseback at all ages. An impressive one of her at the Royal

National Show performing an advanced dressage movement. For a while there dressage had been her passion, until her passion for jewellery making had taken over. Rising Star was a wonderfully supple and responsive ride. Once on the open plain she gave the bright chestnut with the white star on his forehead her full rein.

There was magic in galloping. It was far, far better than driving a powerful Ferrari. One of her male friends had let her take his around a track at high speed. It was exhilarating, but give her a fast horse every time.

A half hour into her ride, when the sunset was turning the deep blue sky into a glory of pink, crimson, and gold with bands of indigo and orange on the horizon, she sighted Luke. He was on horseback, coming from the direction of one of the holding camps. The way he rode filled her with excitement. He was a wonderful horseman. For long moments she was defenceless against the stirring sight of him galloping towards her. Why was she so much in need of her father's love and attention that she took it out on Luke? Maybe if her mother had lived? God how she wished she had. It wasn't all that easy being a child, a young woman, in a man's world.

Luke reined in, his eyes a blazing blue against the golden bronze of his skin. His dark red hair contrasted brightly against the pearl-grey of his akubra. Never a sign of a freckle. Not one.

"Enjoying yourself?" he asked, allowing his eyes to move over her, glossy mane wind-tossed, those beautiful cat's eyes clear and sparkling.

"Yes," she answered shortly when she felt quite emotional.

"How did it go with your father?" he coaxed.

"Well. He asked where *you* were."

Luke made no immediate comment on that. "Let's ride

into the shade. You really should be wearing a hat for protection.'' He glanced at her as she came alongside him. As usual she'd let her hat slide down her back.

"How come you don't get freckles?'' she asked.

He grinned. "You've wanted to know that ever since I can remember. The answer is the same as ever. I don't know. I'm not ginger like poor old Sandy, you know.'' He named a station hand whose freckles were so close together they resembled a mottled tan.

"Dark auburn,'' Storm said, a soft note entering her voice. Luke's mother had had the same beautiful colouring. Any kind of light fired that hair.

"Did you tell him where I went?'' Luke asked, as they rode down on a narrow, curving billabong. The pink and cream water-lilies floating on it were wondrously beautiful and fragile. Like creations in porcelain. Or enamel, Storm thought, her creativity stirring.

"I simply said you went back to work,'' she offered after they'd both dismounted. "He wants you to come up to the house for dinner.''

Luke stared at her for a minute, then turned away. "No.''

"Ouch!'' She glanced at his unsmiling profile. "Would you like to tell him that yourself?'' She gave him a slight, dangerously provocative smile.

"All right I will.'' He bent to pick up a few pebbles. He had to keep his hands off her. He sent them skimming across the water one after the other. "It's your first night home after all.''

"Let's start again,'' she said wryly. After all this had gone on for years. "I'm afraid nothing is complete without you.'' There was no anger in her voice...just a resigned acceptance.

Luke straightened, staring out sightlessly over the dark

emerald lagoon. "It has far less to do with me than a symptom of your father's driving need of a son."

"Do you know I agree with you," she said. "Why didn't he remarry?"

A pause then, "You wouldn't have liked that, Storm."

That unnerved her, threatening her tenuous poise. "Are you saying Dad sacrificed his own desires to appease me?"

"It's possible." He turned at last to look at her. "Having your father's sole attention has always meant a great deal to you."

"And that's not normal?" she asked defensively, staring into his eyes.

"Perfectly normal for a little girl as isolated as you were. Every little girl needs her mother."

She felt such a rush of emotion she turned away blindly. "You're absolutely right." A moment slipped by. "I've tried to get away from you, Luke," she admitted, low-voiced though it seared her.

"I know." His voice equally tense came from somewhere behind her. "I've had to pay a high price for your father's affection."

"How do you mean?" She spun on her heel only to discover him standing directly in front of her. His aura was so powerful, so *male*, she found it intimidating.

"You've figured it out by now," he clipped off. "I lost out on *you*. Your affection."

"Surely it wasn't important to you." Deliberately she moved back a few paces, putting distance between them.

"You charmed me in your cradle." He, on the other hand, stood perfectly still.

"I used to hero-worship you." She found herself saying haltingly as though in the grip of a truth serum.

"Then all at once things changed."

She took a deep shaky breath, trying to suppress the

sharp rising excitement that was cutting through her like a blade. "Dad has ruled our lives," she muttered. "He set us one against the other."

He shook his head. "If he did, he never meant to."

That spooked her. "Why do I ever expect any fairness from you?" she flared. "I can never open my heart to you, Luke. You're always on Dad's side."

"Wake up, will you?" he begged. "I'm here for you, Storm. You might consider it's possible, too, you're never on *my* side. Any chance we could start again?"

"No, I just can't. I really can't," Storm said in a passion. "Too many years have gone by."

"What are you frightened of, Storm?" he asked, fearing his own loss of control. Very quietly he moved towards her, like he sometimes did in her dreams. "Why are you so frightened of *me?*"

She was so alight she felt she would blow a fuse. "Such arrogance!" Her voice rang out caustically. "I'm not frightened of you at all."

"If you back any further you'll finish up in the water," he warned, holding out his hand.

She ignored it, a pulse away from lashing out at him.

"I think you are," he continued.

The air between them vibrated with a tension that had them both catching their breath.

"What do I have to do to prove it?" She stood there, hands on hips, head thrown back, eyes flashing green fire. An attitude of defiance he had witnessed countless times over.

"Why don't you let me show you?"

He started to walk towards her again, his brilliant eyes intent on her, while she tried to fight back excitement and panic.

"Don't you dare touch me, Luke," she warned.

He gave a challenging shake of his head. "I'm genuinely amazed I haven't tried it before. For years you were too young, but you're old enough now. Two fiancés no less."

"I couldn't even count your girlfriends!"

So great was her tumult she actually considered the ignominy of flight. But he was there, one hand taking a fistful of her hair, the other strong arm snaking around her waist pulling her so closely into him she felt the impact of body against body in every last cell.

Luke allowed her to grind against him in a futile struggle, her beautiful, high breasts crushed against his chest, her long-fingered hands flailing wildly. Her breath was coming unsteadily through her parted lips, sweet and clean against his skin.

He lost control.

He was alight with desire. It pounded in his temples and in his brain. The times she had cut him to the bone! The infinite number of times she had played princess of the manor! When his mouth came down over the luscious cushion of her lips, she gave a cry, muffled but keening like a bird's.

"Surely you've been kissed before?" He couldn't stop himself from offering a taunt. The wish to hurt her as she had hurt him was overriding any thought of tenderness. He was unaware his voice sounded drugged with long-denied desire.

Fire crackled, spat, burned through Storm's veins. She'd been kissed many, many times but no one had evoked such a passionate, primitive, reaction. She had imagined him kissing other women. Carla, the rest. In his arms she was forced to admit it, but the reality of having his beautiful clean-cut mouth over *hers* was too overwhelming to describe.

She wanted to lock her lips and her teeth. She wanted to deny him any pleasure he might take from her mouth and her body but the voluptuousness of her own emotions were simply too much for her. It was as if he had taken possession of her.

The very thing she feared.

"Luke, stop!" No order. A plea, knees trembling, her head falling forward against his chest, the wild urge to fight him spent.

"When I'm so enjoying myself?" His resonant voice was husky, mocking.

"What are you trying to prove?" Her skin was pale with the force of emotion, her eyes huge.

"Only the truth," he said quietly, observing her extreme agitation.

"Well the truth is I *hate* you." She responded passionately, on cue.

"Goes without saying! But what do you actually *mean,* given that you kissed me back?"

Storm couldn't bear to consider that. "I did not!"

"Did so. We can play these silly games. You know something?" He put his gleaming head to one side. "You're the greatest kisser I've ever met and Carla's not bad."

She saw red as she was meant to. Luke was an illness, a fever. There was no escape from him anywhere. She moved with feline speed and suppleness. She lifted her hand in an arc, then cracked it sharply against his lean cheek. Fall of flesh upon flesh.

A moment frozen in time.

God! In the heat she felt chilled. Overcome by shame. Humiliation. A kind of despair. She really needed help with no help to be had. Where was the enviable control, the poise that was so much a part of her? It deserted her

utterly on her home ground. As her arm began to fall he
pinned her wrist, not cruelly but leaving her in little doubt
of his vastly superior strength. "A warning, Storm. Don't
do that again. Not *ever*." His eyes were blue stars.

"No I won't." Her tone was full of self-disgust. "It's
too demeaning. And you won't kiss me either. Understood?"

He smiled a little at the "turn the tables" mechanism
she so often deployed, holding her intently with his eyes.
"Now that I can't promise. Not when I've just got a taste
for it."

"Have your little joke," she turned on her heel.

"What makes you think it's a joke?" he called after
her, watching her take the grassy slope like a gazelle.

"You won't like it if I tell Carla." At the top she turned
to threaten him, her cheeks flushed.

For answer he sketched an elegant little bow. "My life
is in your hands!"

It was said with the utmost mockery. A sobering pros-
pect to know it was true.

CHAPTER FOUR

A WEEK slipped away, during which time Storm kept a close watch on her father. His general health picked up having her near. His eyes were brighter behind his glasses. He was always able to summon a smile. He talked endlessly of the old days; how he met and married her mother. How beautiful she was. How much he loved her. How his very existence was threatened when he lost her.

"But I had you, my darling. I had to pick up the reins."

Her father was so happy, so at peace, Storm found it almost impossible to broach the subject of her return to Sydney. Sooner or later she had to. It was necessary to keep her work before the public, especially now when she was riding high on her little moment of fame. But the ideas kept coming. Not just for the swank pieces that brought in the money and had the most staying power, but for good contemporary pieces within the reach of young, sophisticated jewellery lovers. Experimental pieces. She had brought a sketchbook with her—she was rarely without one—and it was almost filled. She'd also been asked to custom-design impressive pieces of jewellery for men. One of her customers was a top male executive who swore by the healing power of carnelian for his legendary quick temper. Others thought turquoise brought good luck. Every gem was credited with a special healing power.

She'd sketched out a few blueprints for bold signet rings either sculptured in solid sterling silver or eighteen carat gold handset with semiprecious stones; lapis lazuli, amber, jade, malachite, opal with its beautiful play of colours, jet, onyx, fire agates. Working with these gems and having easy access to them, Storm felt their power more than most. Diamonds, rubies, emeralds, sapphires and pearls remained the top five. So many legends were attached to them but Storm was just as fascinated by the many semi-precious stones that passed under her eyes. Stones that had been known and used since antiquity. A few years back she'd made a jade pendant on thin-corded leather for her father to wear around his neck. She'd used the most sought after jade, too. An intense apple-green. She'd gone to great lengths to secure it. Jade was said to have healing power over bone problems if it was worn. Her father had taken the pendant in his hand, admired the workmanship, and given it back.

"A man doesn't wear jewellery, sweetheart," he had said in a kindly but dismissive voice. "Besides I don't believe in all that healing stuff."

She still had the pendant at the bottom of her mother's jewel case which was now hers.

Luke became a fixture at the dinner table. Something that worked wonders for the Major's moods, if not Storm's. Luke had the most marvellous calming effect on him. That's what's wrong with me, Storm thought. I'm not calm, volatile mostly. Periods of calm. Always acutely aware of Luke, she had become preternaturally sensitive to his presence. But she had resolved to be good. Pleasing the Major was paramount to both of them. With an effort on both sides, they kept up a charade, a pretence at a new intimacy the Major didn't miss but apparently rejoiced in.

In the daytime Storm took her father for trips around the station so he could call in at the various camps and worksite to speak to his men. Often they enjoyed a mug of billy tea and sometimes a slice of freshly baked damper.

At other times Storm parked the Jeep on high ground so her father could look down on the mob spread out across the plains or a party of stockmen fording them across the shallows of the permanent stream that ran through the station. His favourite port of call was to watch Luke break in the best of the brumbies though "breaking" scarcely described Luke's method. Luke was one of the natural born "calmers."

He had an innate love and understanding of horses. No one on the station knew of one he couldn't ride when horses aren't inherently rideable. The horses Luke handled were broken in superbly. Horse breaking is a highly skilled task. It involves mouthing, riding and educating. Brumbies unlike the station bred horses weren't used to the sight of humans. Station horses were well handled from an early age consequently they were even-tempered and relatively controllable. Brumbies, were something else again. Often their bucking at the riding stage was positively ferocious.

Over the years many a stockman had sustained injuries trying to ride a wild horse; crushed ribs, broken collarbones, broken limbs, broken facial bones. It was a fairly easy matter to get oneself killed, especially if a horse was cornered in a yard. That particular afternoon, the "mouthing" over Luke was riding a big bay standing some sixteen and a half hands with obvious thoroughbred blood. The bay most likely was the progeny of one of the station mares and a brumby stallion. Brumby stallions were notorious for their attempts to run off station mares to join the harem.

"I thought _I_ was good in the old days," the Major grunted in admiration as they sat in the Jeep watching proceedings. "I never had Luke's skill nor patience. He's turned so many of these rogues into good working horses."

"That's the Luke we know and love!" Storm quipped, watching Luke speak quietly, soothingly to the wild horse urging the animal forward. Luke knew better than anyone how to get himself into the horse's comfort zone. Nervous, unpredictable horses were time bombs waiting to go off. Luke knew how to control his own emotions, something that communicated itself to the horse. There were no punishments in Luke's methods. A horse reacted according to its natural instincts he always said. If that presented a problem, then the problem had to be solved.

They sat for a good hour along with several stockmen and the two young station jackeroos perched up on the fence. The youngsters new to Luke's horsemanship were thrilled by the display, one of the jackeroos calling out to Luke for "a go." Luke took no notice whatsoever if indeed he heard the boy. His concentration on the job in hand was too intense. No one had ever seen Luke land on the sand, paralysed with pain.

"Stupid young devil!" the Major snorted with a hard edge of irritation. "Tell him to stop, Storm."

"Okay, Dad. Take it easy. One is foolhardy at that age," she said lightly opening the Jeep door. "I used to want to ride a buckjumper myself, remember?"

"Don't I ever!" the Major said with a faint tremor. "Tell that lad if he can't keep his silly mouth shut he can push off. Go find some work. They simply don't know what's involved here. There are plenty of professional breakers doing the rounds, but I haven't seen one to match Luke. He can control even the most dangerous horse and they're dangerous animals."

Storm walked over to the high railed fence and tapped the jackeroo lightly. "Listen, Simon, keep it down. Calling out to Luke could distract him. That horse could start acting up any time."

Simon flushed. "Sorry, Miss McFarlane." He glanced back nervously to where Athol McFarlane was seated in the Jeep. "It won't happen again. Promise."

"That's okay, Simon." She smiled at him. "We all have to learn."

Luke's session broke up ten minutes after and one of the part aboriginal stockmen took over, an excellent horseman and one of Luke's "pupils."

Luke came out of the yard and crossed to where they were. The Major still seated in the Jeep, Storm leaning back against the bonnet. Father and daughter watched him with varying emotions. McFarlane with pride, gratitude and deep affection, a fatherly love that had turned Storm's world inside out. Storm with the utmost caution overlaid with a kind of emotional tumult that was close to McFarlane's love.

Vibrations came off Luke even at a distance she thought. He had the perfect powerful physique, very lean but in no way thin. Countless images of him were tucked away in her mental file. She thought she'd had it firmly shut and under lock and key but one explosive kiss had torn open the lock. The file lay open although it still seemed important not to look.

"Hi!" Luke acknowledged Storm with the same controlled smile he'd been giving her all week. Even then it had the ability to dazzle her. He walked around to where the Major was seated on the passenger side, leaning in man-to-man.

"I think we've got ourselves a darn good horse, Major. He's a cut above the usual bunch. Thoroughbred blood."

"I'd say he was one of Nahra's." McFarlane of course had spotted it. He named a station mare that had escaped to the wild some years before.

"My guess as well." Luke nodded in agreement. "With

a badly trained horse it takes a good man to work it. Can't have the men flat out trying to handle the horses especially in difficult terrain. That way they won't be able to muster. The bay has potential. Now, what about a cuppa?'' He leaned back over the bonnet to include Storm. ''After that session I'm as dry as a bone.''

''Good idea.'' McFarlane's gruff tones mingled pleasure with approval. ''I've enjoyed this last week immensely. It's a wonder to have Storm home at last. She's been able to drive me all over. It's good to see the men.''

''They're working well,'' Luke assured him. ''It's been a pleasure for them to be able to speak to you, too, Major,'' he reported.

''What about if I have a go at that?'' Storm suggested looking towards the sandy enclosure where the aboriginal stockman was working another brumby. It was a much smaller horse, a filly. The stockman was working from the ground, a technique Luke followed especially when handling a horse with behavioural problems. It was a whole lot safer than trying to work a horse when mounted. Ground control was achieved first before the move to the saddle. Storm whose horsemanship was not in question, found that she wanted to try it. Being home was so utterly different in every way from city life. She loved it. It was so varied and exciting, but she still resented being kept out of the picture.

As it happened it was difficult to say which one of the men said ''No'' first. Her father or Luke. Maybe it was simultaneous.

''I'm not going to get hurt,'' she assured them coolly. ''If Wally can handle it, so can I.''

''I'd rather you didn't, Storm,'' the Major said, his re-laxed expression turning to a frown.

"Fifteen minutes. Luke can watch me. It's just a filly. I can handle it."

"I don't think we could handle seeing you get hurt." Luke spoke quietly for both of them, himself and the Major. "Hazards exist, Storm, you know that."

"You don't say those things to Wally," she retorted.

He considered briefly. "A fortnight ago Wally struck his head on a rail post when a horse bucked high. The filly looks quiet now but she could smash into the rails in an attempt to go through or over them if she takes it into her mind."

"I know," she said in a crisp voice. "I was born here, remember? But I'd like to learn the technique."

"Okay so I'll show you." Luke gazed at this dark-haired, green-eyed "princess."

"That's a promise?" She turned to face him directly.

He struck his heart. "Or hope to die. But we won't be working with brumbies. I can tell you that. You know enough about horses to know any horse can present a serious risk. Let alone a brumby outlaw. Now what about that tea? Take pity on me, Storm." He smiled at her.

It was one of those moments when she felt he reached out and actually touched her. Not just with those beautiful sapphire eyes but his hand. He might have been laying it on her naked breast so erotic was her reaction.

She drew a harsh, shallow breath turning away. "Oh, all right. As far as that goes it's thirsty work just watching you." And waiting...waiting...waiting...for you to kiss me again. Opening the file a little had also opened up a great fissure, a deep, untapped vein of desire that threatened to rock her to her foundations.

*   *   *

The days merged into one another with a continuum of peace. One afternoon Tom Skinner flew in with another physician, a specialist in his field, which was orthopaedics. The door was closed on Storm while both men conducted their examinations and conferred. Her father was an old hand at shutting her out when she was desperate to know the true state of his health. Afterwards, when the two doctors stayed on briefly for a reviving cup of tea, Storm tried her best to get some information. A difficult task when her father sat opposite her finally snapping out testily he was "just fine." Storm drove the doctors to the airstrip, and with her father safely up at the house tried again.

"He's *not* fine, Storm" was all Tom Skinner would say. "He's a very sick man. Life must be hard for him."

"He's dying isn't he." It was a bleak comment, not a question.

Tom stared ahead, as distressed in his way as she was. "Your father refuses to acknowledge such a thing. He's a man who confronts his pain."

"He won't let anyone else do it."

"I know."

"It's rather cruel, isn't it, Tom? While Dad plays the stoic he refuses to let me come close to him." Would she ever get over feeling emotionally excluded?

"It's his way, Storm." Tom Skinner had known Storm all her life and he shook his head regretfully. But Tom was a man under strict orders not to divulge the full extent of his patient's illness. It could be days, weeks, months. Given McFarlane's iron will, a year. "Don't think for one minute you're not giving your father the greatest comfort," Tom consoled her pain.

"He still treats me like a little girl, Tom. You know that. Sometimes I think I can't take it any more, but I can't leave."

"I don't think your father trusts anybody outside of..."

"Luke?" Storm broke in.

"Storm, Luke is as desperate to get through to your father as you are," Tom told her. "In many ways your father is a most difficult man." Obdurate as granite, Tom thought.

Two nights later the crisis came.

Storm woke out of a troubled sleep with a sudden and profound belief something was terribly wrong. She sat up in bed listening as though the house around her would deliver up the answer.

Dad.

Her whole psyche sensed him very near her, like a low beam of light. The sensation was so strong it had her weeping, tears streaming down her face.

Dad!

She flew out of bed, shouldered into her robe, taking the quickest route via the verandah to her father's suite of rooms.

The bedside light was still burning. He was propped up against his pillows. His reading glasses sat low on his nose. His eyes were shut, his mouth open, strong jaw a little slack. The book he'd been reading was still in his hand, pages open.

Sweet God!

Storm just had time to cross herself before she buckled at the knees, falling half-way across the floor. She felt so faint she let her head flop forwards until the dizziness passed. She knew without going a step further her father's mortal life was over. The sensation of his being in her room was his spirit passing.

Finally she rose and approached the bed finding a small measure of comfort in the fact her father's expression showed no signs of agony. He didn't even look tired and worn as he had at dinner. He looked as relaxed as when he was dozing in his favourite chair. He was one of the fortunate ones. He had died in his sleep.

There was no pulse. No breath to fog the little mirror she found tucked away in a chest of drawers.

Storm bent and kissed her father's craggy forehead, speaking aloud. "Go in peace, Daddy. I love you." Her tears fell on his cheek and very gently she brushed them off. Death was such a dreadful shock even when one was expecting it. Never properly understood. Insurmountable to accept.

For a time, she didn't know how long, she sat in a chair beside the bed, holding her father's hand. Her weeping had stopped, though she was trembling so violently, her whole body was vibrating.

Her mind's eye seized on an image.

Luke.

Luke would want to know. Luke could confirm her father's death. Strangely she didn't think of Noni. Not yet.

Storm let herself out of the front door into the darkness of the night. A cold wind was blowing in from the desert but she was oblivious to it. The sky was ablaze with a million stars. Another one up there tonight. Up there in the Milky Way, the home of departed heroes.

She wasn't wearing slippers but she felt nothing underfoot. She continued along the drive, through the gardens and out into the compound to the first of the staff bungalows, a glimmer of white. It was the biggest and the best. Home to the station's overseer. She passed a bank of honeysuckle on the way, its perfume so sweet and haunting it would always stay in her memory of that night. Resolutely she moved on, seeming to glide in her filmy nightclothes, long skirt stirring and floating on the night wind.

She moved up the few steps to the verandah. The bungalow was in darkness but she didn't hesitate. She knocked on the door.

"Luke. Luke." Her voice unknown to her, rose in a poignant wail. In the depths of her grief she only knew she wanted him.

Inside the bungalow Luke came out of an uneasy sleep.

Was he dreaming? He was certain he heard Storm's voice. Nothing unusual about that though. He dreamt about her frequently. With a groan he fell back against his pillow only to hear the voice come again. She was right outside his door. For an instant his whole body froze. Only one thing could bring Storm to his door.

Even as he thought it he was up, pulling on jeans. He didn't linger long enough to grab a shirt. She was standing outside the door, staring up at him, eyes unblinking even though he had switched on the porch light.

"It's Dad," she said, her voice so soft he had to bend his head.

"Oh, Storm." He reached for her and folded her into his arms. *"Storm."* His mouth found the top of her head. Kissed it. Drank in the fragrance of her hair.

"He could have told us he was dying," she murmured brokenheartedly.

He held her and rocked her saying her name gently time and again. "Don't talk about it now. It's all over." She seemed barely conscious her face and mouth were against his bare chest, but even in the deep distress of the moment his body reacted. "I'll come up to the house with you." With sheer force of will he pushed back all sense of desire.

"Would you?" She lay her palms flat against him, lifting her head to stare up into his face.

"I'm always here for you, Storm." He could have

added: I've always loved you. But even in grief he had his pride.

It was the start of over one hundred hours of purgatory for Storm through which she suffered deeply. Finally Athol McFarlane was laid to rest in the family cemetery on Sanctuary Hill. The funeral had been delayed for several days with her father—that lion of a man—laid out in a cold room, until mourners from all over the country were able to organise travel arrangements to the remote station; extended family, life-long friends, important people within the industry, pastoralists, politicians. They came by charter plane, private plane, a whole convoy of vehicles that made the long, hot trek overland. All of them determined to pay their respects to a fine man, to the McFarlane pioneering dynasty.

Luke had taken charge, making all the arrangements. Storm had let him, too grief stricken, too wretched, too disoriented to get herself together for the task. She had no one now. She had never known her mother. Her father was gone. Totally orphaned at twenty-seven.

Luke knew how she felt. He had lived half of his life that way.

Only on the day of the funeral did Storm regain control. Perfectly dressed in an outfit that had to be flown in as was his, a two-piece black suit, lustrous pearls at her throat and her ears, black pumps on her narrow feet, her long hair drawn back into a coiled pleat, a black hat with a down-turned brim on her head. Luke marvelled at the transition from brokenhearted child to woman in control. Only once at the graveside did she buckle but he had his arm beneath hers to support her. Somehow they got through, though Luke could feel the agony in her.

Up at the house, though he stayed near her, she seemed

in perfect control of her emotions, but her beautiful skin that had taken on a golden glow after her weeks in the sun had a tell-tale pallor. Mourners approached her to offer their sympathy and she spoke to each one in turn, her face sad but never betraying the full extent of her anguish. That was for later. Noni and her helpers circulated, offering platters of finger food and sandwiches. Tea and coffee was served, as well as cold drinks and spirits for the men. The men expected it as her father would have expected it at a friend's wake. No matter what, people had to be fed. Most of them had come a long way.

Carla Prentice, who with her parents had attended the funeral as a matter of course, waited her moment to get Luke alone, the depth of her jealousy startling herself. For at least an hour he had hovered around Storm like a body-guard, his attitude clearly protective. As if Storm needed any protection. Carla seethed as she stared across the packed room to where Storm was standing talking to the Davisons, a wealthy pastoral family. Storm had taken off that very becoming hat—too becoming for a funeral Carla thought—the severity of her tightly pulled back hairdo un-expectedly flattering. It showed off the perfection of her profile and the long swan neck. A very cool one was Storm, Carla thought, her throat tightening, eyes flinty. What made her think she was so superior? Why did people approach her the way they did? Anyone would think she was royalty.

Karen Prentice joined her daughter for a moment, her voice flat with warning. "Take that scowl off your face, Carla. It's most inappropriate."

Carla brushed her curly hair from her forehead. "I'd no idea I was scowling," Carla retorted, a light flush staining her cheeks.

Her mother's voice was low and toneless. "My dear, you're looking at Storm as though you hate her."

Was she? Carla felt instant shame. "Sorry, Mum."

Her mother took her hand. "Don't think I don't know how you feel. Luke is overdoing it following Storm around. But then she has no-one really."

"She has plenty of friends," Carla pointed out, her voice strained. She was unable to take her eyes off Storm and Luke. Luke was talking to Senator Austin but he was only a few feet away from Storm. Even in the heat when most of the other men had removed their jackets, Luke still wore a beautifully tailored black suit, his black tie sombre against the snowy-white of his shirt. Carla didn't see him formally dressed that often, now she gazed at him with such longing it seemed too much to bear. How handsome he was.

She could hear the sound of his voice, dark with a little edge to it, so attractive her mother always said it was just plain seductive. It had certainly seduced her. No other woman had snatched him from her grasp and a lot had tried. When Luke had appeared interested she had taken a few necessary steps. Lied if she had to. Carla felt a wave of self-disgust sweep over her. She had never imagined she could act the way she had. Falling in love with Luke had made her a little crazy. Even Storm had the notion they were friends when Storm was the enemy, beyond competition. When Storm was around everything changed.

A woman close to Carla was weeping quietly, comforted by a friend. Carla felt like weeping, too. Not for Athol McFarlane. For herself.

Senator Austin moved off leaving Luke momentarily on his own. Carla came out of her spell to rush to his side, clutching his arm.

"Impossible to believe the Major has gone." Now she allowed a few tears to come into her eyes.

"Yes." Luke sighed deeply, looking over to Storm's slender black-clad figure. "There's a lot of grief facing Storm. I know how I feel. Bereft. The Major was kindness itself to me."

Carla nodded. "I know he was, Luke, but you were worth your weight in gold to him. These last few years you're the one who's been running Winding River. My big thought is how is the Major going to express his gratitude?"

"Meaning what?" Luke's voice was a little hard.

"Come on." Carla hugged him gently. "Don't get me wrong, Luke. I only mean the Major is sure to mention you in his will. For that matter what is going to happen here on the station? Storm has her own life in Sydney. She's anything but a countrywoman now. I expect when she's feeling better she'll return there."

"We haven't discussed anything, Carla. It's been such a shock even though we all knew the Major was ill. But Storm is her father's daughter. She'll make the right decision."

"She'd be mad to let you go," Carla said wholeheartedly, forced to face the danger.

"I may well be looking for something else myself," Luke surprised her by saying wryly.

"Really?" Carla's gold-brown eyes opened wide. Hope stretched before her. "You could just about walk into any job you liked. We all know you could handle the top job on any station no matter how big. And you're such a great businessman!" She sparkled up at him and pressed closer.

Luke made no response to that but said quietly, "I think Garth Fullerton wants to have a word with me. Would you excuse me, Carla."

"Of course" came the gentle reply. "I've been waiting to speak to Storm. My heart aches for her. Now might be the moment. That Isabelle person has been monopolizing her for ages."

"Storm, darling," Carla cooed, when she reached the other young woman's side. "Why don't you come and sit down. You've been standing such a long time. Could I get you something? A cold drink?"

"Ye-es, please, Carla, if you would." Storm was grateful for Carla's intervention. Isabelle Parish was a very nice woman, but she did tend to go on.

Carla, loathe to give up her place, put up a hand to signal one of the house girls who arrived with a tray of cold drinks. "Orange all right, Storm?" she asked.

"Mineral water if there's any." Storm sank into a chair, wondering if she could last much longer.

Carla put a glass into Storm's hand.

"Thank you, Carla."

"You're so pale." Carla was torn between genuine sympathy and self-interest. "Is there anything I can do for you? You're so brave. Everyone admires you."

"What else *can* I be, Carla?" Storm asked, the usual colour missing from her voice. "Dad would expect me to conduct myself well. Even at his funeral."

No tears, thought Carla judgementally dismissing the depth of Storm's feeling. In reality Storm was in shock, numb with disbelief.

"There must be hundreds here," Carla said, almost brightly, looking around.

"So many good people." Storm was struggling to hold onto her exemplary control.

"Luke has been a great support to you," Carla pointed out, a little awed by Storm's beauty and dignified manner.

"Yes, he has," Storm acknowledged. "I don't think I

could have endured it without him. He's shielded me from so much.''

Carla was tempted to say: *Far too much.* "I can understand you're very glad he's here. In a sense you'll be lost when he moves on.''

"What?" Abruptly Storm came out of her grief-induced haze. "What did you say?"

Carla could see quite clearly she was disturbed. "I'm sorry...I haven't upset you, have I?" she begged. "I thought Luke would have told you he has plans to move on.''

Storm felt the ground had moved beneath her feet. "We haven't spoken about anything, Carla," she said, her throat gone dry. "Has Luke spoken to you?"

Carla hesitated, a pitying look in her eyes. "Luke and I discuss most things, Storm," she confided gently. "You must know we've grown very close?"

Storm nodded. "Of course." Luke had known Carla for years.

"It would be impossible to hold onto Luke anyway," Carla continued kindly. "I know he considered he was under a tremendous obligation to the Major—the Major being so good to him—but now the Major's gone."

"You sound as though that makes you happy?" Storm looked up from the contemplation of her empty glass. Even through the pall of grief and depression she could sense Carla's inner coldness and dislike.

"I'm happy when Luke's happy," Carla said, reaching over to pat Storm's hand somewhat patronisingly. "We can be serious now about our future."

"What stopped you being serious before?" Lacking in energy though she was, Storm faced Carla, at the same time removing her hand.

Carla appeared not to notice. She glanced over to where

Luke was standing in sombre conversation with other cattlemen. "Luke has had such close ties to your family, Storm." Her voice held faint disapproval. "I mean it's really extraordinary the way your lives have become entwined. You could almost be brother and sister."

Storm felt a little of her unnatural control slip from her. She stared back. "What nonsense, Carla." She shook her head. "Luke has never been a brother figure to me. I'm sure he'd tell you I've never been any little sister to him, either."

"Maybe not." Carla seemed to blanch at the expression in Storm's green eyes. Suddenly she regretted what she had started. "But you are bonded in a way. I'm only saying with the Major gone Luke is free to lead his own life."

"He's always been free, Carla," she said.

With a huge effort Storm rose steadily to her feet.

By late afternoon everyone had left. Private planes, charter planes, helicopters including a large Sikorsky helicopter belonging to a multimillionaire grazier, charter buses, 4WD's. Storm had retired to her room but found she couldn't lose herself in sleep. It would be hard enough when night finally fell and she had to get through those long, melancholy hours. Tom Skinner had left her with a sedative. If the worst came to the worst she would take that. For now she changed into her riding clothes and went down to the stables where one of the boys, seeing her coming, saddled up Rising Star.

She wanted to gallop to the ends of the earth. And beyond. Frightened of the searing grief that was in her; frightened by what Carla had told her. So Luke wanted out? Whatever happened between them, she'd always believed he would stay.

Why? She needed to face the fact she had been an arrogant, complacent fool. When had she ever shown her appreciation for all Luke's hard work, his many skills, not the least of them that visionary business brain, his loyalty and devotion to her father? Why had she ignored him when he said he would never work for her? She had grown used to Luke as a fixture in her life. As if Luke for all their differences would always be there.

What have I done?

On this day of days she had never wanted to hear she could lose Luke. Luke was too important. Not only to Winding River but to her.

She turned towards the endless mulga plains, then gave the mare her head, urging her on as though the two of them were hell-bent on winning an important race. They took an old broken fence, relic of a holding yard, she, perfectly still and balanced, as Rising Star soared over it athletically, comfortably clearing the top rung. The next one they came on, the mare, responding to Storm's reckless mood, took it at too much of a rush. Power and speed took them over but it had been a near thing. Storm chastened, eased up, her heart thudding.

Her father had gone from her life. In one fatal stroke she was on her own. Now Carla was telling her she and Luke had plans. It didn't seem possible Luke could make that kind of commitment to Carla then kiss her as he had done. Maybe it had been anger, accumulated years of resentments, but there had been passion there. On both sides, the depth of which had shocked her. She'd been perfectly well aware Carla had been pursuing Luke for years. Carla was a stayer, one hundred per cent committed to a particular course of action. Luke was a catch in any woman's language even without a family dynasty and everything that went with it. Power, influence, money. Carla's father was a very wealthy man. Rich girls could marry poor guys if the guy had much to offer. Like Luke. Luke would fit very nicely into the Prentice operation. It was big enough to accommodate two sons and a dynamic son-in-law.

It couldn't be true! She couldn't make sense of it. She had seen Luke and Carla together, sensed they had once been lovers, but it was an attraction that had gradually died. On Luke's part, she'd thought. She kept remembering people did marry for money. It happened all the time. Many a wedding she had attended weren't exactly love matches. They were well-considered social and business contracts. And they seemed to work when romantic love as a sole basis for marriage was often not enough. Carla, though she appeared so open and direct, was a woman of wiles. A calculating woman. Luke had talked about starting up his own operation. Banks weren't lending as they used to. He would need a lot of money behind him. Or a rich father-in-law?

That wasn't Luke. She had come to see Luke in all his facets. Except one. As a lover. Storm sighed deeply. It seemed she had spent her life in self-deception....

She was overlong getting back to the homestead, not caring she had strayed into the hill country. If dark fell and she had to spend the night in the wild she would have a few dingos for company. She was dimly aware of riding into the lit stables, one of the boys helping her dismount, taking the reins from her, all the time speaking soothingly as if to an invalid. She couldn't describe how she felt. Numb wasn't an appropriate word. There was too much pain there, just barely papered over.

Half-way up to the house Luke, walking very purposefully, met up with her.

"Thank God you're home." His voice was worried. "I've had a couple of men out looking for you for the last half hour. Where were you? Not in the usual places, that's for sure."

"I don't honestly know. I was straying."

"Straying is dangerous. Don't ever go off without telling us where you're heading."

She could feel herself tensing. "Ah then, but I'm the boss remember?" It was the worst tack to take but she was dreadfully off balance.

"I don't care who you are," Luke said, locking her with his gaze. "You can't leave worried people behind you."

"I'm sorry, Luke. I appreciate your concern." The answer was truthful, edged with just a little touch of jarring irony. It was too well ingrained.

"So you're coming back to the house?" he asked.

"Nowhere else to go."

"You've barely eaten for days," he pointed out, the note of concern still in his voice. "You'll have to try something."

"I suppose." For an instant she felt like throwing herself into his arms. She was so weary. "It just doesn't seem to want to go down my neck."

They had reached the front steps, Storm starting up them slowly, Luke standing perfectly still on the drive looking up at her. "Aren't you coming in?" She couldn't bear to be without him.

He didn't miss the inflection of dismay. "If you want me to." His voice was a little rough.

"I don't want to be on my own tonight," Storm said and she didn't care how it sounded.

CHAPTER FIVE

THEY ate in the kitchen. Noni, fighting her own deep distress, had been sent off with her friend, Ellen, to take a break from so much trauma. Always a tower of strength, Noni had appeared close to breakdown, too vulnerable to insist on staying which she considered her duty. It was Luke who convinced her he would be there to support Storm.

After her ride, Storm took a long shower letting volumes of precious water pour down on her head in an effort to rid herself of the anguish that threatened to break cover. Thank God Luke had come for her when he had. She would never have forgiven herself had her father died without her.

"Dad!" Her voice was thick with emotion. She simply couldn't absorb it.

Afterwards she sat quietly at the table watching Luke going about the business of making them something to eat. What am I she thought? A child? But she'd come to a crossroad. She was aware as well she had always been subject to intense emotions. Luke hadn't even asked her what she wanted to eat, realising she didn't much care. He moved with such supple grace. A man totally at ease with his own body. At ease with himself.

After a while she got to her feet to find plates and cutlery. Luke had already thrown a clean white cloth over the Victorian pine table with its four Windsor chairs. Now she replaced the large fruit filled silver bowl centre table, breaking off a couple of grapes and placing them absentmindedly into her mouth. The kitchen had a lot of atmosphere, comfortable and friendly in contrast to the formal rooms of the house, which were overly grand, enriched by splendours her forebears had acquired at some stage. Occasionally she'd had notions of redecorating, weeding out certain objects and pieces of furniture but her father had been adamant the house had to stay as it was.

"Now it's all mine," she murmured aloud. No joy in it. A statement of fact.

"The big thing is what you're going to *do* with it?" Luke asked quietly, adding dressing to the salad and tossing it until the various greens were lightly coated.

"God knows! It can't go out of the family."

"Unthinkable!" he said. "Isn't Bloomfield coming back tomorrow?" He referred to the family solicitor, senior partner in the firm of Bloomfield, Bloomfield and Merrick.

Storm nodded. "I asked him to stay over but he said he had things to discuss with Scott Cunningham. Mr. Cunningham is a client as well. Anyway I'm in no frame of mind to hear Dad's will. Are you?" She shot him a glance that burnt out of her pale face.

"Just take it quietly, Storm," he advised, pouring lightly beaten seasoned eggs into a hot pan that was foaming with a little butter and oil. She could smell the fresh scent of the parsley and snipped chives he had stirred into the mixture.

"You're certain to be mentioned," she said in a matter-of-fact voice.

"Does that bother you?" He glanced over his shoulder.

"Of course it doesn't. You deserve far more than a mention for everything you've done. Dad wasn't the easiest of men but you always knew how to keep the harmony."

"It wasn't difficult." With the omelette coming together

Luke sprinkled the surface with grated parmesan. "This looks good. I expect you to eat it."

"You're quite a dab hand at making omelettes." She watched him fold it with the ease of an expert turning it out onto a warmed plate and sprinkling the top with a little more parmesan.

"It's the ultimate fast food. It's nothing to work a fourteen-hour day. I needed to master something simple and quick."

Storm sat down again, contemplating the pattern in the damask tablecloth. "Perhaps that says a lot about you, Luke. You master anything you turn your hand to."

They ate in near silence. Luke poured some wine. "What are we celebrating?" Storm asked, her eyes seeking his. Part of her was deeply disturbed, the other part surprised at how good the omelette was; how fresh the chilled wine tasted on her tongue.

He studied her a long while. She was wearing not a skerrick of make-up, eyebrows, eyelashes like black velvet, skin flawless, her mouth a natural tea-rose. But her eyes were dark with intensity. "You need to unwind a little, Storm. A glass or two of wine will help relax you."

"I have to make sure it does." She sipped a little more, staring across the table at him, this unique man who was woven into the very fabric of her life. "I want you to know how much I appreciate all you've done for me these past days," she said a little raggedly. "I thought I could run my own life but losing Dad has been like a great earthquake." Her hand tightened on her glass, until the knuckles showed white.

"I understand," he said quietly. He felt pretty much the same way.

Another silence, stamped with tension.

"And when did you propose to tell me about your

plans?'' she fired at him much later, her voice so brittle it cracked a little.

"What plans?'' he countered, disturbed by the tremor in her hands.

Storm hesitated a moment, appalled by the thought she might cry. "I may have this wrong but I gathered from Carla you only stayed on for Dad. Without him you'd planned to move on.''

Something near anger burned in him, showed itself in his electric glance. "When did you learn this?''

She rubbed her eyes a little desperately. "This afternoon.''

"You mean Carla broached the subject today of all days?''

"I don't think she could resist it. Is it true?''

He reached across the table and grabbed her trembling hand, his fingers very tanned against her ivory skin.

"Why would I discuss my plans with Carla before talking to you?''

"You tell me?'' God how her heart hurt!

"I'll tell you it sounds darned odd. Can you *ever* believe in me?'' His voice was taut.

"I'm sorry. Are you saying Carla is making it all up?''

"I guess I am. Carla isn't above pulling a few tricks. I could cite a case,'' he began, but switched off. "What was your conversation about?''

"Lord, Luke.'' She nearly laughed. "About you. Carla says among other things you and she have made a commitment to each other.''

"Have we really?'' he said, almost amusedly, the overhead light ringing his dark red head with fire. "I think Carla finds the odd lie downright useful.''

"You haven't?'' She looked at him questioningly, relief welling inside her.

It showed. "You make it sound like it's very important to you." He gave just a glimpse of his beautiful, illuminating smile.

"It *is*." Her voice carried sincerity. "I know I've said a lot of things in the past—I was wrong—but I couldn't do without you. I couldn't run Winding River, let alone the whole operation. Dad made a point of keeping me sidelined. I had to turn my attentions, my energies elsewhere."

"And in doing so discovered your own talent," he replied, hoping he meant a hell of a lot more to her than a highly valued employee. "You're a creative person, Storm. Designing and making beautiful jewellery must give you a sense of accomplishment?"

She nodded. "It does, but now I'm left with one of the biggest cattle operations in the country and I know next to nothing about it."

"You can learn."

She held up a hand. "*Can* I?"

"You're a highly intelligent woman. The big question *is* do you *want* to run a string of cattle stations?"

At the thought fatigue washed over her, she swallowed, feeling the great weight of her new responsibilities. "I'd like to know as much as I possibly can. Besides who could I trust to run it outside you?"

"Actually you could find someone," he answered more crisply than he intended, the urge to take her in his arms so powerful he nearly buckled under it.

"I don't want to."

What was he? Overseer, business manager? Nothing *more?* "I don't know that it suits me to walk a couple of steps behind you, Storm." He saw very clearly how that might be.

She raised her beautiful shadowed eyes with the first sign of anger. "You mean you won't work for a *woman?*"

"I mean I won't work for *you*," he answered without a pause. "You know too well how to make it tough for me. We've had a very stormy relationship. Just like your name."

"I was jealous of you, Luke. You can't possibly know how it was." She sat back in her chair, pushing her freshly washed hair over her shoulders. "I could hear myself shouting but it was like a voice in the desert. Dad had such power over me and he used it. To my shame I have to admit I was terribly jealous. But you wouldn't turn your back on me now? You wouldn't leave me when I desperately need you?"

He stared into her black-fringed emerald eyes. "When my life to date has been Winding River? I'll stay on until I can find someone to take my place. I'm not irreplaceable, Storm."

She gave a little wry smile. "Dad seemed to think so and he would know. I'm not about to crawl even for you. I don't want to insult you, either, but I have no idea what Dad was paying you."

"Storm, darling, a lot," he drawled, tossing off his wine.

"Knowing Dad you must have earned it," she retorted, her heart jumping at the endearment even if it was sardonic. "I'll pay more." What was she doing talking about *money?* The mistress in the Big House! Without Luke she'd be lost in more ways than she could yet imagine or fully understand.

"Don't let's talk about this tonight," he said.

"Why not?" She met the molten blueness of his eyes. "It diverts my mind when I'm full of grief and panic. Were you *ever* in love with Carla?" She had struggled not to ask that, but lost the battle.

"That's my business," he pointed out calmly, the light falling on his clean, chiselled facial bones.

But once started, she found it difficult to stop. "I thought it was all over. She says it's not."

"I thought your involvement with Alex was over?" he countered, preserving his cool front in an excess of strong emotion.

"It is but that doesn't mean we're not still friends."

"The same goes for Carla and me." He shrugged.

Restlessly she pushed her plate away, her heart labouring. "You'd better tell *her* that. She's madly in love with you, Luke."

He heard the combined note of worry and jealousy with a rush of pure joy. "You know I think you're probably right but I made no promises to Carla."

"You *were* lovers?" She put it to him too fervidly, betraying the extent of her own involvement.

"And you and Alex and the guy before him weren't?" he asked dryly. "Don't let's get into an argument."

She bit her lip, then shook her head. "Not me. I'm going to be good from now on."

He reached over, caught her hand and lightly shook it. "Well then, you can try. We can't go on as we did before. You know that, don't you?" His voice was deep, quiet and steady. It carried great conviction.

Some of the great pain eased within her but she didn't answer. Storm hadn't yet learned to reveal her secret heart.

The wine made her drowsy; gave her a few hours heavy sleep. She awoke in the early hours, thinking she heard footsteps; her father's heavy, uneven tread along the corridor before he retired for bed. She sat up quickly, for one long, dislocated moment thinking the last terrible week hadn't really happened. It had all been a nightmare. If she got up now, opened her door and called to him, "Everything all right, Dad?'' he would answer, "I'm fine, darling. Go back to bed."

Except he would never speak to her again.

Storm found the bedside light switch, her breath ragged over the trip-hammering of her heart.

"Dear God!" she said aloud. It was neither a prayer nor an outpouring of despair. Perhaps a bit of both. The digital clock read 1:40 a.m. With trembling fingers she pushed back the top sheet and the light coverlet walking through to the ensuite and turning on the light. She was bone-white, her eyes bruised and shadowed. She turned on the cold water, splashed her face several times, patted it dry, drank a long glass of water, then began to retrace her steps. Chanting carried on the wind. She listened with a kind of wonder. The aboriginal people who moved freely across the station had organised their own wake. Athol McFarlane had always treated them so well and respected their culture.

It was a beautiful moonlight night but Storm was almost blind to it. She padded out onto the verandah listening to the mournful singing from the camps. It had stopped at some point but started up again. Death, the final crisis of the life cycle, was always associated with ritual, she thought. For the white man and the aboriginal. In the Dreamtime death wasn't always inevitable, but someone in the beginning had taken the fatal step that set the precedent; like the story of Adam and Eve. Like her own people death, too, despite belief in an afterlife, was an extremely upsetting affair for the aboriginals. Athol McFarlane's death had affected every last man, woman and child on the station and the news had been communicated far in the desert tribes. The mourning ritual had gone on for many hours of the burial day, but after the wailing a great stillness would fall over the bush. The chants weren't only to accompany her father to the spirit world and see him safely settled, they were meant to give comfort to her. In a way they did but the mournful singing marked by clap sticks and sand drums added to her acute emotional distress. She found her heart breaking and breaking all over again. Grief would stay a long time in her veins.

Desperation carried her down the verandah to the large guest room where Luke was sleeping. There had been no talk of his returning to the bungalow. Storm hadn't wanted to be alone; Luke was very upset himself, so it had been agreed without words that he would stay in the house.

She cared nothing for her flimsy attire, too distracted by her need for comfort. The only person in the world she could look to for comfort now was Luke. Luke had known her all her life. Her father had loved him like a son. Probably in ways she as a female could never have attained. At any rate, more than her. But Luke at this moment was her only salvation. He, too, had been dealt a terrible blow by her long-adored father's death. So at the end a very complex but unbreakable bond held them fast.

Luke woke out of a fitful sleep to see her framed in the doorway.

For an instant he was blinded as if by an apparition. The radiant moonlight streamed through her long gauzy gown, delineating the lovely curves of her body, edging them in silver. Her wonderful glossy raven's wing mane tumbled over her shoulders dishevelled by sleep. She was the absolute essence of woman, the beauty, the mystery, the boundless allure.

While he watched spellbound she called pleadingly. "Are you awake, Luke?"

He felt like saying he was immediately awake every time she came into his orbit.

PLAY BANGO! AND GET THREE FREE GIFTS!

It looks like **BINGO**, it plays like **BINGO** but it's **FREE!**

HOW TO PLAY:

1. With a coin, scratch the Caller Card to reveal your 5 lucky numbers and see that they match your Bango Card. Then check the claim chart to discover what we have for you — 2 FREE BOOKS and a FREE GIFT — ALL YOURS, ALL FREE!

2. Send back the Bango card and you'll receive two brand-new Harlequin Medical Romance™ novels. These books have a cover price of $3.99 each in the U.S. and $4.50 each in Canada, but they are yours to keep absolutely free.

3. There's no catch. You're under no obligation to buy anything. We charge nothing — ZERO — for your first shipment. And you don't have to make any minimum number of purchases — not even one!

4. The fact is, thousands of readers enjoy receiving our books by mail from the Harlequin Reader Service®. They enjoy the convenience of home delivery…they like getting the best new novels at discount prices, BEFORE they're available in stores…and they love their *Heart to Heart* subscriber newsletter featuring author news, horoscopes, recipes, book reviews and much more!

5. We hope that after receiving your free books you'll want to remain a subscriber. But the choice is yours — to continue or cancel, any time at all! So why not take us up on our invitation, with no risk of any kind. You'll be glad you did!

YOURS FREE!
This exciting mystery gift is yours free when you play BANGO!

Visit us online at
www.eHarlequin.com

The Harlequin Reader Service®—Here's how it works:

Accepting your 2 free books and gift places you under no obligation to buy anything. You may keep the books and gift and return the shipping statement marked "cancel." If you do not cancel, about a month later we'll send you 4 additional novels and bill you just $3.34 each in the U.S., or $3.74 each in Canada, plus 25¢ shipping & handling per book and applicable taxes if any.* That's the complete price and — compared to cover prices of $3.99 each in the U.S. and $4.50 each in Canada — it's quite a bargain! You may cancel at any time, but if you choose to continue, every month we'll send you 4 more books, which you may either purchase at the discount price or return to us and cancel your subscription.

*Terms and prices subject to change without notice. Sales tax applicable in N.Y. Canadian residents will be charged applicable provincial taxes and GST.

"Storm, what's wrong?" He got up very fast, the moon illuminating his lean, hard body, naked except for a pair of navy boxer shorts.

"I know it's crazy, but I'm a little scared. I thought I heard Dad's footsteps coming down the hall."

He didn't blame her. It was a very strange night and the chanting at the camp was so melancholy it could push anyone over the edge. "Your father would never hurt you," he said gently. "It's your overwrought mind playing tricks."

"Oh, Luke," she said. "I can't believe he's dead."

"Do you want to go downstairs?" he asked, his blood running hot just looking at her.

"I want to stay here. Can I? I won't bother you in any way."

Her voice was as sweet as a little girl's. My God, could she really believe that? But helpless tears glittered in her beautiful eyes.

"Sure." He spoke with a kind of asexual comforting tone. "You take the bed. I'll take the armchair over there. You'll probably need your own pillows. I'll go back and get them." He went to move out onto the verandah but she plunged almost desperately past him into the room.

"I want you to put your arms around me. It's wonderful sometimes to have a man by your side."

He could have groaned aloud but he didn't. "Hey, Storm, this is going far beyond our usual exchanges. I can handle them."

"I've been awful to you all my life but I'm going to make it up to you. Carla even said she thought of us as almost brother and sister."

"Yeah?" he rasped. "Carla was simply trying to fool herself and she's no fool."

"All right, I know it's never been like *that* but you're

the only one I've got. I'm only going to lie down." She turned towards the bed and slipped beneath the thin cover. "Look at it, it's big. There's plenty of room. I'll be myself again tomorrow. Promise."

To take advantage of her would be the ultimate betrayal. He knew he could *never* do it. To his utter horror he agreed. "Okay. You're going to have to go off to sleep now because I have to make my usual pre-dawn start. No matter how terrible this week has been the work never stops."

"You've made it endurable," she whispered, as he moved onto the bed, lying down and tucking his arm beneath his head, his heart knocking so loudly against his chest surely she must hear it, but she turned her body towards him, a sorrowing child again, not a woman aware of her own extraordinary power. She lay barely covered by the thin sheet. He made extra sure he lay on top of it, though if it were an iron barrier, his body temperature would have melted it.

"Good night, Luke," she said softly, lifting her head slightly and kissing his cheek. "You couldn't be cruel to me if you tried."

She wasn't faking anything as another woman might have done. Not Storm though she was very seriously in need of him. His silence, however, contained grief, wonderment and the fiercest inflammable frustration that kept him very still, every muscle rigid with tension. He was a man like any other man. Not a superman. Didn't she know anything might set him off? A slender arm flung across his chest in sleep? Her satiny face burrowing into his neck? The scent of her assailed his nostrils, full of so much allure, so much sexual intoxication, he made a near infinitesimal movement of withdrawal.

She stirred. "Oh, Luke, don't pull away," she begged,

her heavy eyelashes already falling. Pull away? When he wanted to bind her so tightly she would never get away!

It took her two minutes to fall into a light sleep, her body relaxed, as though she knew even in her subconscious being with him kept her safe.

He loved her of course. He loved her fire. Her quick temper. He loved her in all her dimensions; the sweetness, the zest for life, her artistry. He loved her capacity for deep feeling. Her love of the land. He even loved the flashes of lightning that went off when they were on the verge of a huge argument. It was impossible to capture her yet here she was in his bed, sleeping on his shoulder, his arm going a little numb from supporting her head. It could fall off for love of her, he thought. Damn you, Storm!

Ten minutes later he dared to look down at her sleeping face. She was fast asleep now, lashes still. The room was almost stage lit bathed in moonlight. The deep V of her lace trimmed nightgown revealed the exquisite shape of her breasts. By this time he was feeling a little wild and he was a man who had long since learned tight self-control.

Time to move to the chair. But she seemed to feel his intentions even in her sleep. She flung out one arm just as he feared, turning her body further to be nearer his.

God, you've got to help me through this, Luke prayed. I'm a decent man. But I'm a man in love.

So appealed to, God heard. Eventually Luke slept.

Storm opened her eyes with a start, wondering briefly, wildly, where she was. The air hung with a pre-dawn silence that would soon be dispersed by the songs of a trillion birds. A soft, misty light was entering the bedroom, pearling down on her and a man's long muscled back, the skin polished bronze, velvet in texture. He was turned so

far away from her he was on the very edge of the bed.
The head on the snowy pillow glowed like a dark flame.

Luke.

He looked utterly beautiful. A marvellous man. She'd
been afraid of him for most of her life, so powerful were
her feelings of coming second best. The mystery was how
she had retained so much confidence in her personal worth.
She and Luke hadn't got on at all. She knew now it was
because she'd always been in jealous competition for her
father's attention. It was her father's doing; though he had
been genuinely unaware he was causing such damage. The
result was she had elected to take it out on Luke. Himself
a victim of tragic circumstances.

Desire such as she had never known spiralled in her.
Up...up...making her feel light-headed. She wanted to
stroke him, so badly she couldn't control it. Her fingers
reached out, feathering along his skin. It seemed like some
kind of miracle—he was here with her until she recalled
she had begged him to stay in case her grief and sense of
dislocation carried her away.

"Luke..."

She held her breath, her fingers deepening the pressure,
so she was caressing his warm flesh.

He came awake at once, slicking his hair back with his
hand. He turned towards her, with such a rush of joy it lit
him up like a torch. Such naked longing was in her beautiful green eyes he didn't hesitate. He pulled her down to
him with strong, powerful arms, pressing her to him.
Blinding desire drove out any other consideration but having her. God hadn't he imagined it? Too frequently. *This*
was unstoppable.

"Luke—"

Just saying his name was a release. Her voice broke, but
he muffled her murmurs with his mouth, kissing her so

deeply and in such a fashion, she gasped once forbidden little endearments into his mouth, her fingernails digging into the bare skin of his back.

Inhibition vanished like puffs of sand on the desert wind. "I want you desperately," he muttered, his voice half smothered by her cushioned lips. "Lord, don't you know that?"

She tried to draw back a little, overwhelmed by the magic, her cheeks flushed with body heat. She stared into his taut face, her eyes enormous, dark green. "Make love to me, Luke," she whispered. "I can't fight you any more." The haunting was over.

If only that were true! He wished it with all his heart, but doubt pursued him. He had lived through long years of rejection by this beautiful creature.

But she kissed him. A kiss that transcended his fears. The initiative entirely hers, the kiss lingered on with such bewitching seductiveness he felt the blood beat hot and heavy in his veins and pool in his loins. He would never forget the touch of her lips, the irresistible softness, the satiny texture. His hands moved compulsively in a great, primitive yearning to know her body, finding first the pearly mounds of her breasts, feeling the wild beating of her heart beneath his palm. Her nipples were tightly crushed berries, the electric tingling his fingers induced in her, transmitting itself to him.

To be with her was ecstasy. He felt as though he was drowning in a tumult of sensation. That in itself was a frightening thing. For him to give so much power to this woman. It was an enormous risk yet he was so violently aroused, in such a frenzy of intoxication; he was unable to resist the magnitude of the temptation. There was no past. Perhaps no future. He only knew there was the here and now.

She was reciprocating, her slender limbs spread and writhing in a high state of excitation as he went about exploring her body passionately, deliberately, intimately. She was perfect. Everything he had ever dreamed about. He would always have her...if only in his dreams.

Excitement mounted to a kind of rage. Delirium. He could hold back no longer, the hard trembling starting up in his arms. But he had brought her to the very peak of rapture so she was guiding him irresistibly into her body, her movements swelling, her rhythm matching his. He was taking her away; far into that enchanted world inhabited only by lovers.

The rising sun brightened the sky. Rosy light stole across the bed, bathing the beautiful, naked bodies curved and fused as one.

CHAPTER SIX

WONDERMENT shielded her from the worst of her grieving. The residual mists of magic clung to her through the morning and helped her rejoice in the celebration of *life*. After the dawn's transforming experience she had fallen asleep, awakening long after Luke had left. She hadn't had a chance to speak to him about how she wanted him to be in attendance at Robert Bloomfield's visit. However, it had been agreed over supper the night before he would greet the solicitor at the airstrip and drive him up to the house. Senior partner in the family firm of Bloomfield, Bloomfield and Merrick, Robert had been her father's solicitor ever since she could remember. He would arrive in time for lunch. After that they would retire to her father's study where Robert would read the will. Storm wanted Luke to be with her. Luke was sure to be a beneficiary. He had a right to be there and she would probably have some expert advice.

Storm felt certain of the will's contents. Bequests to charities, extended family members, goddaughter, two godsons, lifelong employees, that sort of thing. Certainly Noni would receive something. Noni had been a wonderful support. But the bulk of her father's estate, which had to be considerable—though she had no real knowledge of his affairs—would go to her as his only child. She had no great interest in becoming a very rich woman probably because she had been an heiress all her life. Privilege was part of her background, not that she didn't thank God every day for it. She would continue the practice of family philanthropy. Get involved.

She went about the business of preparing lunch, dreaming a little, feeling guilty as though she had had no right to dream with her father so newly dead but the height of intimacy she and Luke had attained had given her strength. She set the table, three places, in the formal dining room, overlooking the rear garden with its groves of native trees, dense plantings of agapanthus and silver and grey foliaged plants all of which withstood the rigours of the Dry. A small pond fed by an underground spring was full of perfect water-lilies the colour of the sunrise. Tiny black native bees hung like clouds above the huge blooms drunk on the nectar. She could smell the heady perfume as it floated through the open windows.

The station was synonymous with water-lilies. They floated every billabong, every lagoon, their beautiful showy heads standing high above the water, the blue, the violet, the purple, the exquisite fragrant pinks and the hardy white with their deep golden centres. She stood for a moment staring out, a little awed by the depth of her feelings, wanting to protect them. They were so very new, so tender, like a newborn babe. Feelings only Luke had been able to call up so effortlessly.

Their lovemaking had been breathtaking, full of intense excitement, surprises and blood rushing need. Her shattering climax had been totally unfeigned. He had played her body like the most sensitive instrument in a master's hands.

She had never known anything remotely like it and she was a woman who had imagined herself in love at least twice. It occurred to her how contemptuous, however benignly, her father had been of all her male friends, especially the men she had allowed herself to become engaged to. She thanked God now she hadn't done them much harm. Paul had another love interest, a fellow woman barrister who would suit him far better than she ever would; Alex was hanging in there, thinking persistence would win the fair maiden but she realised now she had fallen in love with Alex for the most superficial reasons. He was good-looking, good company, intelligent, ambitious, but she knew he hadn't even begun to tap into her body's needs, let alone touch her soul.

Time now she stopped betraying herself. Time she stopped the self-deception. Her accumulated resentments, her flawed perceptions had all but robbed her of Luke. Her father in championing him, showing his deep regard and admiration had perversely turned her in many a wrong direction. Time all that was stopped.

But what of Luke? Even at the height of passion, when not only their bodies but their souls were naked, neither had uttered one word of love. Surely her endearments had been so frantic as to be incoherent? Luke had told her he wanted her. She had revealed in every possible way she wanted him. Needed him desperately.

Surely that was love?

The word whispered aloud, quivered like a butterfly on the delicate petal of a flower. All this she found soul-shaking. Her feelings were so profound they scared her. Love was the most precious commodity in the world. The most talked about. The most desired. Once given it put great and dangerous power into the hands of the beloved.

The beloved! There was no terror in whispering it to herself. Luke, the beloved. Her love for him had taken root long, long ago but it had never been allowed to bloom. The high fence for her now was finding the courage to allow it full growth, full expression. Did one learn that overnight or were all the defences she had built up too strong to be knocked over at will?

One thing was certain. Luke being the man he was would not brook any continuation of her former touch-me-not behaviour. How ridiculous she seemed to herself now. The haughty little girl, the even haughtier adolescent, the cool cutting woman.

Shame on you, Storm.

The grandfather clock in the hallway chimed noon. It brought her out of her reverie. Robert Bloomfield was due to fly in within the next half hour. Everything was in readiness. Nothing elaborate. That was inappropriate. Tarragon chicken salad with a handful of shelled walnuts thrown in. She'd made it and refrigerated it a couple of hours before. No Noni to bake fresh rolls. There weren't any left in the freezer, either, so she had to make up a batch of little dampers sprinkled with poppy seeds. Noni had taught her a few things. The little dampers were delicious with or without butter. Even if Luke, unprepared, couldn't stay for lunch she hoped he could be on hand for the reading of the will.

She was waiting on the verandah when they arrived, a cool vision in white linen with one of her own beautiful silver belts with turquoise and agate beads roped around her small waist.

Robert Bloomfield, a substantial, clever-looking man with a shock of prematurely white hair and contrasting very dark eyes, mounted the short flight of steps to greet her. "Storm, my dear! How are you?" It wasn't simply social lubrication. The answer really mattered to him. He had known Storm all her life. Long sympathised with her vulnerable position as a lone little motherless girl in what was essentially a tough man's world. His dear friend,

Athol, had always sought to protect her but he treated her like a fragile exotic flower instead of a desert rose. Storm in reality was as hardy as they come. As she would have to be once she learned the contents of her father's will. If she so chose it was contestable, he would be willing to represent her.

Storm was raising her cheek for his kiss. "A little better today, thank you, Robert. I hope the trips back and forth haven't been too tiring for you?"

"Not at all, my dear." He turned his distinguished head to include Luke, whom he liked and admired enormously. But still…?

"I didn't want Luke going to the bother of having to bring me up to the house. I know how pressured he is even at a time like this." Station work as he well knew never stopped. Dawn to dusk sometimes into the night. Seven days a week.

Luke gave him his white shining smile. "No problem." But he shifted his gaze to Storm, his feelings so intense they blazed out of his eyes. Hours later and he still felt as though he were intoxicated. Their fusion was still imprinted on his body. The magic so potent he thought it would never fade. "I'll be off now. You're okay."

Storm didn't care acute disappointment sounded in her voice. "Couldn't you stay to lunch, Luke? I'd so like you to."

"I'll second that," Robert Bloomfield spoke up, approval on his face. "I'm sure there's much to discuss."

"That would be great but I don't think I can spare the time," Luke apologised. "The rains have started up North. Flooding already. The floodwaters will eventually feed into our river system. For that matter we could have flooding here."

"So it's all hands on deck for the bit muster." Robert

Bloomfield nodded, understanding the situation perfectly. "Perhaps later on in the afternoon, Luke?"

Luke tipped his wide-brimmed akubra. "I'll try to make it up to the house before you fly back, Robert."

"But aren't you coming to hear Dad's will?" Storm found Luke's eyes almost pleadingly. "I'm sure you'll be mentioned."

"Maybe." He shrugged. Hell he deserved something but not if there was going to be any fallout. "It all has to do with you, Storm. I'm not family."

"And you're not just a valued overseer either. Please, Luke, I need you."

It was the first validation of caring Robert Bloomfield had ever heard from Storm and it set him back. As long as he could remember Storm and Luke had shared a very prickly relationship. Of course it was all Athol's fault. The man should have remarried. He'd told him so. Had sons. In McFarlane's world sons were viewed as the big assets. Daughters were the decoration. Bloomfield was aware he had taken sides long ago. His sympathies to this day were with Storm. Consequently he waited on Luke's answer with some trepidation.

Luke put a considering hand to his jaw, obviously trying to work out how he could find the time. "Can you give me a good hour?" he asked. "Maybe an hour and a half."

"Surely," Robert Bloomfield agreed, when truly, he didn't think it was a good idea at all.

They ate a companionable lunch, afterwards walking around the home grounds. They were absolutely extraordinary to Bloomfield's eyes, especially in relation to the vast wilderness beyond. Yet the landscape designer called in at the turn-of-the-century had had the great foresight—in a time when gardeners persisted in trying to plant delicate exotics—to design a magnificent native garden that conveyed a great sense of place. Over the years more in Athol's mother's time—Lady McFarlane had been a passionate gardener—the vision had expanded. He remembered as a young man marvelling at the regiment of gardeners who laboured along with the remarkable Mistress of Winding River to create ponds from subterranean streams planting the water grasses and the magnificent water-lilies that in all parts of Queensland grew like weeds except these weeds took the breath away with their beauty.

There were no sweeping lawns and garden beds of bright beautiful flowers such as his own garden in Brisbane. The homestead's extensive grounds kept to the natural contours and extraordinary flora of the desert environment, with a few introduced exotics that could withstand the conditions. Yet the flowers here seemed to smell more sweetly than anywhere else, he thought, inhaling their fragrance which carried for miles. The native boronia! Glorious! It had to have something to do with the dryness and heat releasing all the aromas.

It was a very pleasant interlude tinged with the to be expected sadness. It wasn't long after they found their way back into the house that Luke arrived. He must have decided to take a quick shower and change his clothes because he was dressed in a plain navy T-shirt with a white logo across the front, light blue jeans, his dark, fiery head damp from the shower. He was a very striking-looking young man, Bloomfield thought, looking across Athol McFarlane's huge partner's desk at him. Those handsome chiselled features, the stunning colouring. But over and above that he was a man of the future. He had the brains, the toughness, the natural authority that was God-given, to run the huge McFarlane operation.

Only one thing. He wasn't McFarlane's son. McFarlane's natural heir. Storm was. Bloomfield didn't think Storm was about to celebrate the news he now commenced to read out.

It was just as she expected, sitting side by side with Luke in leather armchairs. Bequests to various members of the McFarlane extended family; a large very valuable painting of an evening landscape by a famous early colonial artist was to go to one of Athol McFarlane's longtime mistresses. Forever kept in the background, out of respect to the memory of his wife, she was now handsomely rewarded. A range of charities were also to benefit handsomely; a collection of rare first edition books were to go to Robert Bloomfield himself, a sterling silver tea and coffee service dating from the latter part of the eighteenth century to his wife, Gillian, who had been bridesmaid at Athol McFarlane's ill-fated wedding.

Then came the crux....

Storm listened with a sense of total disbelief, so shocked she looked outwardly calm. How her father loved playing games! How transparent his motives! All her life she'd been led to believe she would inherit Winding River along with its two outstations now Robert was telling them in a completely dispassionate voice she and Luke had been accorded an equal share.

"I don't believe this!" she interrupted after a while, shaking back her heavy hair. "Didn't Dad know what this means?"

The temperature in the room had shot up for all the ceiling fans.

"I'm afraid he did, Storm," Bloomfield looked over the top of his glasses as they slipped down his nose. "Luke is to be granted what is termed a life estate. This means..."

"I know what it means," Storm said with a return to her old fire. "It means that Luke has half share in the station for his lifetime."

"After which it passes to you should you outlive him, to your issue or appointed heir," Bloomfield concluded, himself shocked by his friend's actions.

"Good God!" Luke sighed so deeply it seemed to consume his splendid, lean body. "Whatever made him do it?"

Storm swung her head, her eyes startling green. "Surely that's obvious? He had no faith in me. Any male at all would be an improvement on a woman. *You* were a natural godsend."

"Don't blame me, Storm," said Luke, picking up a glass of water and drinking from it.

"I'm *not* blaming you," she cried, recognising she was. "This is a dilemma, Luke. What are we supposed to do? Share the homestead, share the profits?"

Bloomfield coughed, lowering his eyes to the printed page. "Actually, Storm, as Luke is expected and indeed *has* to continue working the operation *he* gets the profits."

It was too much for Storm. She jumped up, her cheeks firing with colour. "What! I can't possibly accept this. God, Dad must have hated me."

Luke fixed his eyes on her. "Sit down, Storm," he said, making Storm and the solicitor witness to his tough side. "This bequest is for the sole benefit of the station. But you don't have to accept it. If you feel an overwhelming urge to contest the will, go for it."

Storm felt she was in grave danger of bursting into hysterics. "God in Heaven!" she said, but managed to sit down quietly and cover her face. "People are going to start to wonder if you aren't in fact Dad's natural son."

There was a brief silence while Luke's brilliant gaze whipped over her. "I'll forget you ever said that," he said in a deadly quiet voice.

"I'm sorry," Storm apologised. She had shocked herself. "But could you blame anyone for talking? Can you blame me for wondering what the hell is going on?"

Bloomfield looked across at her beautiful, passionate face. "I do think it was too bad of your father not to explain all this to you young people. I know it has come as a great shock but you see what he was getting at...Luke summed it up. You couldn't at this stage run Winding River yourself, Storm. You'd have to get in a full-time manager and a darn good one at that."

"I could fix that." Luke was sitting straight now.

Bloomfield shook his head. "For someone else to come in was the very last thing Athol wanted. He wanted *you*, Luke."

"My God didn't he!" Storm's little laugh broke. "He couldn't have made it any plainer." Inside she felt as if she was being pulled in all directions.

"Luke has carried the whole operation splendidly, Storm," Bloomfield pointed out. "You must give him that."

"Of course I'll give him that." Storm clenched her hands. "Luke is extremely capable like his father was before him. Dad relied on Luke even more heavily. I know what Luke can do, but God!—" She broke off, devastated.

As was Luke who felt quite stunned. "This looks like heading towards another nightmare," he said. "What happens, Robert, if I renounce this bequest?"

"Your share passes to Storm, of course," Bloomfield informed him, suddenly seeing what a bad move that might be. Especially for the station.

"Then Storm can have it," Luke said, rising to his feet. "And while she's about it she can find another overseer. I can give her a couple of names."

Storm swallowed hard, trying to get herself together. "What's wrong with you?" she demanded, thinking she was losing her right arm. "Why are you on your high horse? Did you expect me not to be shocked? You're shocked yourself. Or *are* you?" The minute the words were out of her mouth she bitterly regretted them; a legacy of all those years.

Luke ignored her. "I'd offer to drive you back to the airstrip, Robert, but I'm sure Storm can attend to that. If you'd excuse me I was paid up until the end of the month so I'll get on with my job."

"Don't you want to hear the end of it," Storm cried to his back.

"No, thank you very much." Luke swung around to answer quietly. But there was no way his inner anger could be missed. It burnt out of his eyes and showed itself in the pallor beneath his golden-bronze tan.

There was total silence in the study after Luke had left. Bloomfield holding his heavy head in his hands, Storm fighting a tidal wave of tears.

"He has his pride, my dear," Bloomfield finally pointed out quietly. "That was an unfortunate remark you made in relation to prior knowledge. You know what a secretive man your father was. If he hadn't lost your mother I'm sure he would have been quite different. In fact he was as a young man. But losing your mother changed him enormously. It wasn't inborn. I do know he adored you.

"Perhaps not in the way you wanted but according to his own lights. Women have such a wonderful refining influence on a man. I bless the day I met my Gillian. I can't imagine what my life would have been without her. Your mother would have given your father a well-integrated, happy life as she would have given you. With the best will in the world your father didn't know how to go about it."

Storm looked at him with great sadness. "That's not the

case, Robert, if you look at his relationship with Luke. Even before Luke lost his parents Dad thought the world of him.''

Bloomfield nodded his head. ''Well, Storm, it must be said, Luke's that kind of a young man. Let none of us forget he did save your father's life. It greatly reinforced the attachment.''

''Of course but it wasn't enjoyable for me. I wanted to be brave and strong like Luke. Not Dad's pretty little girl. Luke and I are so terribly enmeshed. I know it was dreadful of me to say people would wonder if he weren't in fact Dad's son, but Lord, Robert, you know as well as anyone Dad idolized him.''

''And you bitterly resent that?'' Bloomfield asked quietly, thinking it might have broken someone else.

''I did,'' Storm said, ''but I thought I had confronted it, Robert. None of this is Luke's fault. But I'm too far gone casting him as the scapegoat.''

''Except he's scarcely that,'' Bloomfield reminded her. ''If you allow me to finish reading the will, Storm, you'll find that your father left you a very rich young woman indeed. You don't need the income from the cattle operation, I assure you.''

Storm considered that carefully. ''The money is not the point, Robert. It's the whole principle of the thing. Even from the grave Dad set Luke above me.''

Bloomfield looked understanding but pained. ''I wish you wouldn't see it like that, even though I do understand. I can't find a nice word for this, but I'm afraid you have to consider your father was a master manipulator.'' He spoke very seriously but Storm gave a poignant smile.

''I know that. Luke and I have even talked about it. Dad manipulated us both. He's still at it.''

''The perfect solution would be for the two of you to

marry,'' Bloomfield suggested, emboldened by what he had seen on his arrival.

"Oh, Robert!'' Storm started up, staring at her own portrait. What a haughty piece she looked. A real firebrand. Was she really like that? "Luke and I have never had any romantic involvement.''

"Are you sure of that?'' Bloomfield asked gently. "Gillian and I always thought you set one another off. I don't think, my dear, you've ever given Luke half a chance.''

Storm turned. "Luke isn't a half a chance person. It's all or nothing with him. I don't deny I've fought him for most of my life. Fought off his enormous hold.''

"So you are attracted to him?'' Bloomfield watched her carefully.

Her expression gave her away. "The very minute I start to get things into perspective something like this happens. I never in my wildest dreams thought Dad would *handcuff* us together. I loathe it.''

"I'm absolutely certain, although he never said so, your father intended the two of you to marry,'' Bloomfield offered.

"That would solve everything, wouldn't it?'' Storm replied with false blitheness. "Especially in regard to Winding River. Luke could run it. I could produce the next heir. After all that's a woman's job, isn't it? Having the babies, raising the kids. I had a career. Not that Dad ever saw it as one.''

It was sadly true. "Surely you can continue your career, Storm,'' Bloomfield said. "You're brilliant and very widely sought after. Gillian loves the beautiful necklace and earrings you created for our twenty-fifth wedding anniversary. I love to see her in it. Surely you can work from anywhere even if you have to make business trips from time to time?''

''What are you suggesting, Robert? Luke and I should bury our differences and get married.'' The very thought took her breath away.

''Whom you marry is your business entirely, Storm,'' Bloomfield pointed out. ''I wish you all the happiness in the world. You have had every material want but I do realise in many ways you were emotionally deprived. Luke, too, for that matter. He lost his parents at a very vulnerable age.''

Storm dipped her head. ''And he never acted up. Not like me. Luke took it on the chin. Whatever he thinks of me, Robert, whatever the bond, Luke isn't a man I can twist around my little finger.''

''Not like the last guy, eh?'' Bloomfield gave her an owlish smile. ''What was his name?''

''Alex. He's still around. He won't know about Dad. He's in Hong Kong on a business trip.''

''But that's all over, the relationship?'' Bloomfield asked, looking at her a little sharply.

Storm shrugged. ''It wasn't really ever on. I've never found the man to satisfy me.'' Outside Luke, she thought. Luke had brought love-making to a fine art.

''I take it Luke's romance with the Prentice girl didn't amount to anything?'' Bloomfield continued very smoothly.

''Not for her want of trying. She's madly in love with him.''

''So would I be if I were a young woman.'' Bloomfield gave a little bark of laughter, then swiftly sobered. ''What are you going to do about Luke, my dear,'' he asked quietly. ''You realise you could contest your father's will. My firm will stand by you.''

"You believe I have a right to?" Storm asked in a tight voice.

"Most people would." He shrugged. "Athol could have left Luke a sizeable sum of money. Enough to kick-start a small operation. Luke has all the skills to build on that. He's a young man with a big future."

"And besides he has half of Winding River. Off the record, Robert, I don't want you to speak as a lawyer, but as a family friend, what do *you* think I should do?"

Bloomfield considered very carefully. "This is one you have to solve yourself, my dear," he said finally. "I'll back you whatever you do, but this cuts too close to your heart. I suspect to Luke's as well. You *are* the main beneficiary of your father's will. There's plenty more left of it to read. You and Luke share Winding River at least in Luke's lifetime. After that, as I said, it reverts to you or your heirs. Luke cannot take up a position anywhere else— I'm darn sure Clive Prentice would love to have him sign on at Mingari—but under the terms of your father's will he has to stay here and run the whole operation. For that he takes the income, which I suppose is fair enough. Being a top cattleman is hard, dangerous work and one has to have a natural rapport and authority with the men. So far as residing together in the homestead, that's something I can't possibly decide. God knows it's big enough to house a small army but there are the proprieties of course."

Storm was vibrating with nerves. "I've offended him deeply," she said. "It's one of my hang-ups."

"I'm afraid, my dear, you have. But knowing you I expect you can smooth things over. Angry or not I know Luke cares a great deal about you. I watched the two of you at the funeral. It seemed to me you share a very strong bond, whether you want it or not. Now sit down, again, Storm, so I can get on with reading the rest of the will. At the end you'll find yourself a lot better off than even you expected. In fact you'll be one of the richest young women in the country.''

So why didn't it cheer her up? Storm slipped quietly back into her chair.

When Robert left she would have to find Luke. Not to kiss and make up. Her father had just made him her honorary brother.

The mauve dusk came and went. Night set in. Luke didn't come up to the house. Not that she had been expecting him to. He was probably as shell-shocked as she was, but her feeling for him erased everything else. In the starry darkness the desert air was cool and crisp. It enveloped her. Lights were on at the bungalow and she mounted the steps marvelling how swiftly events had overtaken her. Her father's death; the funeral; her night with Luke; the power and passion of their union when they had both forgotten their place in the scheme of things.

Now this. The will. Just as their relationship flared into sexual radiance everything could crumble. Maybe there was even something inevitable about it. Like a doomed affair. She anticipated Luke would be uncharacteristically cold but when he opened the door to her knock so casual was his expression she might have been one of the station hands. ''May I come in?''

''If you wish.'' He was the picture of calm but he was angry. She knew it. It was all in his eyes. And she knew those eyes.

''Have we really come to this, Luke?'' She looked around the living room, which was comfortably, even cosily furnished, spotlessly clean and tidy, but smaller than her own bedroom at the house.

"I haven't got the answer to that question, Storm," he queried. "Are you going to sit down?"

"Thank you." She moved to a club chair. "I didn't handle the will reading very well."

"Truth to tell neither did I." He glanced towards her. She was looking all of a sudden very fragile in that masculine chair. "Have you had anything to eat?"

"I had some lunch."

"I was making coffee. Do you want some?"

"Yes, thank you."

"So what have you come to tell me?" he asked a little later, placing their coffee on the table between them along with a ham sandwich. "Go on, eat it," he prompted.

She felt too sad and weary. "Why did Dad *do* this, Luke? Help me understand."

"Why?" His cleanly defined mouth tightened. "No matter what you think not to enrage you. Your father lived his life as the man in control. Scott Fitzgerald once said that the rich are different, and it's not just that they have more money. Your father had the power to control lives. Whatever he wanted had to happen. You must know he had plans to marry us off."

"No, I didn't," she answered at once. "All I know is every single male friend I brought here he compared unfavourably with you. Surely he didn't think that was the right way to go about it?"

He frowned slightly. "Eat your sandwich."

She shook her head but picked it up and bit into it, surprised to find she was hungry.

Luke let her finish it before pushing her cup of coffee nearer her. "Like another?"

"You're definitely, but definitely a carer. That was good but I'd rather talk right now. Dad seems to have made you my honorary big brother."

Luke responded instantly losing his cool. "The hell he did! The things you say, Storm. You're really something."

"Must be one of the reasons you love me." She smiled at him, very wryly, trying to lighten the mood.

"Why would I love a terrible woman like you?" he said in the same wry tone.

She stared at him with intensity. "God knows!" She held her head. "Maybe I'm disturbed. Maybe we can't live without one another. Situations like this must exist."

"It's the strangest case I've ever struck," he returned dryly. "The person who made things so easy and so difficult for us was your father. He should have had a son of his own."

"I'd still have been shunted into a back seat," Storm said, knowing it to be true.

"But you wouldn't have resented *me* at all. I wouldn't have been part of the equation."

She shrugged. "Anyway, it's all hypothetical. I knew Dad would reward you for your hard work and dedication...I expected that."

"But you never expected he'd do something so intolerable. You do find it intolerable, don't you?"

Storm drew a jagged breath, unable to deny it. Even from the grave her father was affirming Luke's value as equal to hers. "Can't you understand it's been a blow?"

"Of course I understand." The words burst forth. "I've been understanding all the injuries to you for most of my life. We've been presented with a dilemma, which I understand can only be resolved if we marry. Simple, if we were so madly in love with each other no problems existed. But marriage is a pretty big hurdle."

"You wouldn't *marry* me?" she asked, acknowledging a perverse sense of outrage.

It brought an ironic smile to his mouth. "The only way

I'd want you to come to me is of your own free will. But the handicaps are very much in place. The Major has put me in a bad position. You might consider that.''

''In what way are you in a bad position?'' she retaliated, thinking they would be forever locked in conflict. ''Overnight you have half of Winding River.''

There was an endless, endless pause filled with a ringing tension.

''I thought I made my feelings pretty clear,'' Luke said, blue eyes electric. ''You can stick Winding River, ma'am. Get your boyfriend Alex to run it. Contest the will if you like. Argue undue influence I coerced your father into leaving me half the station. He was in very poor health. A dying man very largely dependent on me, not only to run the whole operation but for company. You sure as hell kept *your* distance.''

It was a struggle not to hit him, but she didn't make that mistake. She stood up, anger and anguish all over her face. ''I was wondering when you were going to say that. I've been dreading it actually.''

''Why not?'' his voice was hard with mockery. ''You go ahead and blame me for everything no matter what. The sad fact of the matter is you can *never* trust me. You'll always be harking back to days that would have to be left behind. That's where this feeling of *powerlessness* you have began.''

That did it. ''So what are you suggesting, peace at any price? What am I supposed to say, Luke, good on you. You *deserve* half my inheritance. Bighearted Storm. I think it's lovely Dad thought so much of you.''

''Hey,'' he said. ''I told you. I don't want it.''

''Then you're a fool.'' She tried to pull herself together, her anger shaming her by tipping over into desire. ''Only it's not so straightforward, is it? You're not a fool. Far from it. You know I wouldn't contest the will.''

Suddenly Luke could take no more. "I think if you don't want to risk getting manhandled, you should get out of here.''

She wasn't even the heiress now. "You don't scare me, Luke. I happen to know you. You're nothing if not the perfect white knight. Whatever I think of this arrangement, it was Dad's decision to split the station between us. He knew I couldn't work Winding River without you.''

"Try to concentrate when I speak to you,'' Luke said, sounding very tough. "That isn't a consideration. I told you I could find you someone very capable to take over. Two names come to mind. I'll give you both.''

"You won't stay?''

"Obviously this needs spelling out in big letters. N-O.''

The hardening of his mood, the things he was saying, somehow frightened her. But she wasn't about to show it. "You've been paid up until the end of the month. You said so yourself.''

"Okay but I won't wait a minute longer.'' He clipped off the words.

"You'll refuse Dad's request?'' She was thoroughly unnerved.

"Maybe you should just *go,* Storm.''

"All right.'' She had her pride. She walked to the door, her eyes huge and brilliant in her pale face. "Dad felt you were crucial to our continuing success. I can't deny I'm finding this hard, but I think so, too. We both need longer, Luke, to think about all this.'' Deliberately she met his condemning eyes.

As if she were tormenting him he thought. She looked quite heartbreakingly beautiful. So much a part of him. Even at this worst of times he wanted her desperately but he would fight that to the death. One thing he'd learned: Storm had an infinite capacity to hurt him. "Good night, Storm," he said resolutely. "It's been one hell of a day."

"Tell me about it." She made a little sound like a sob. "What happened to us last night, do you know?"

He stared at her from his superior height. "You're all grown up, Storm. I guess it was sex."

She took a ragged breath. "Is *that* what it was?"

"*You* need to answer that. I couldn't."

"It wasn't just sex for me," she confessed, very softly as though she was speaking to herself. "It was *incredible*. Like something I've never known."

It would be madness to weaken. "Well I guess now it's all over," he managed to say coolly. "Sad for me. Sad for you. But that's the way it is."

Blindly she turned away. "I think I'll go back to Sydney in a day or two."

He nodded, cut to the heart. "Well that's what you were going to do anyway, wasn't it?"

She was quiet for a moment. "I feel dreadful," she said firmly. "I can't believe what's going on."

"It's absolutely clear to me. The thought of sharing Winding River with me has upset you dreadfully. As if you weren't upset enough already. I'd have been a lot happier if your father had left me his damned stamp collection."

She was too disturbed to smile. "He *did*. If you'd waited you'd have found out. There are other things as well. Personal things," she said despairingly. "You didn't even ask…"

"How very rude of me." He simply couldn't bear to look at her and not take her in his arms. "I'll walk you up to the house," he said briskly. "Are you going to be all right on your own?" Even now it worried him.

"What in a house where Dad's haunting every corner?" She shivered in the crisp night air.

"You always did have too much imagination."

"Unfortunately, yes." She breathed out audibly in mute appeal.

"I think we can work something out," he found himself saying. "You sleep in the bungalow. I'll go up to the house."

She raised her dark head. "I don't know." But she did know. She wanted to. Even if Luke wasn't there.

"So that's settled." He read her eyes. "You can collect a few things at the house then we'll come back here. I'll leave from the house in the morning, otherwise I would have to wake you." He had a sudden vision of her asleep beside him that very morning, brushing it down, but not the monstrous deep ache inside him.

"Thank you, Luke," she said quietly, like a sweet little girl. "It's such a very, very *big* house and it's so filled with *him*."

At this point of time it was true. "What it needs," he said tautly, "is children. Lots of them."

"Oh, Luke." There was a little tremor in her voice. "I was thinking four." Sudden tears appeared.

That was his undoing. He gave way to the awful, tearing desire that was rising in him. He pulled her into his arms, so hard, he was certain it hurt her but he didn't care. He wasn't going to be overshadowed by that other dominant male figure in her life. Her father. He wasn't going to let anyone else have her.

Storm, too, felt the waves growing, curling over into great tunnels that were taking her under. She clung to him, frantic for more, only he released her abruptly, keeping hold of her shoulders.

"Whatever man you choose to father your children," he said, his voice harsh with emotion, "you're going to lead him one helluva merry dance."

CHAPTER SEVEN

THE bungalow had good karma. The instant her head hit the pillow, Storm fell into a deep dreamless sleep. Not even the birds woke her; her nervous exhaustion was so complete. She'd slept in Luke's boyhood bedroom that had charm and peace about it. She remembered the display cabinet in the corner. His mother had bought it to install in his room. It was filled with sporting trophies he had won at school and university. Luke had been, still was, a superb athlete. He excelled at polo but as her father's health failed he'd found less and less time to play it.

Three guitars hung on the wall.

She took one down and began to tune it, staring out the open window at the cascade of white bougainvillea like a bride's veil. She and Luke had once fancied themselves as musicians. They had entertained themselves, her father and friends who came to visit the station, with country and western songs, which always went over well. It had amused them a lot. They weren't half bad in those far-off days. Their voices had blended well. Still in her nightgown Storm sat down on the bed again and began to strum an old Irving Berlin song about loving somebody always...always....

Of a sudden she stopped playing, unbidden tears gathering in her eyes as she acknowledged Luke had *always* been there through the best and the worst of it. There was more joy, more pain, more anger, more *passion* in being with Luke than anyone else in the world. Just as there had *always* been the struggle to accept him. She'd been en-

gulfed by her feelings; she was nothing beside Luke. In
her city persona, she had become a confident, successful
woman—much admired. On her home ground she was still
the immature teenager whose great underlying wish to be
number one with her father was never fulfilled. Not then,
not now, not ever but she remembered Robert's words—
her father had loved her in his fashion. When was she
going to accept the circumstances of her life? When was
she going to rise above the past? She had her own identity.
She was a woman and revelled in it. She might have
wanted to be a boy when she was a child, a tall, strong,
clever boy who could easily compete with Luke for her
father's attention. Now it seemed pathetic and well...sad.
She was totally happy and secure in being a woman. In
fact she was quite unable to contemplate her old primitive
wish to be a boy. It seemed so ridiculous now.

Sometime she had to start a new life. A life free of her
father, adored though he had been. Surely it was time? Her
heart might still ache at the wounds of the past but she
would have to let them heal. Her father obviously hadn't
even considered her feelings in leaving half the station to
Luke. Maybe he had even thought she was willing to share.
After all he had left her a very rich woman. But in giving
them each an equal share there was so much potential for
conflict. They would have to marry to make it work.

She mulled the situation over long enough to agree with
Luke's taking the profits. He would, after all, be in charge
of the whole operation. He would do the work though she
was darn sure she was never going to be sidelined again.
She wasn't a fool, a butterfly by nature. She ran a business.
A good business that was expanding. She'd had clients fly
in from Hong Kong, Thailand, California, all over to have
her design something special for them. All the things she
should have been taught about Winding River's operations

she was going to learn. Not that she'd encounter the same problem with Luke. She didn't doubt for a moment Luke would show her everything she needed to know. Luke was a man of today as opposed to her father who had always maintained she didn't really need to know anything about "business" and became quite rattled if she persisted. Even rattled with Luke who could do no wrong. Luke had often tried to include her in discussions but both of them saw clearly it had irritated Athol McFarlane too much.

Men were men and women were women and never the twain should meet. Except in bed. Athol McFarlane's thoughts on having a woman, even a daughter, as a business partner.

So she was going to drive Luke away? Knowing Luke it could happen very fast. What if he turned his attention to another woman? What if he married her? Would the new woman then become part-mistress of Winding River? She, herself, would be expected to make her residence in Sydney, visiting very infrequently. Luke had his share for life. The income for life. After that, if she survived him— somehow she couldn't bear to dwell on that—his share would revert to her. So in the end Winding River would come to her children.

Rather than start up a headache, Storm took a quick shower, dressed in the clothes she had brought from the house, a yellow T-shirt, above the knee cargo shorts, white socks and sturdy boots. She knew the aerial muster was going on today. Luke would be flying the helicopter. She'd find a good vantage point in the hill country and oversee the muster. She always found it thrilling. Afterwards she could do a bit of prospecting, picking up her stones. She'd found many a piece of opal matrix in the ancient hills. She might be lucky again today. She shoved her yellow akubra on her head, drank a glass of milk from the refrigerator and picked up a couple of shiny red apples. She'd be going some distance so she'd take one of the Jeeps.

Sometimes the station used the big helicopter operation run by Grant Cameron, other times Luke took up Winding River's reliable Bell 47. Luke was a high-calibre pilot. Heli-mustering in a tough industry was both cost effective and a time saving alternative to stockmen in a big operation like theirs. A half hour out she spotted the red helicopter flying low over the scrub. It was flushing out hundreds of cattle and rounding them up. Stockmen on the ground were working in conjunction with the helicopter, on motorbikes and horseback. If this year the rains a thousand miles to the tropical north of the state continued, or a cyclone swept in, this vast riverine desert would go underwater. The plains were so flat the water could spread for fifty miles. In this part of the world it was possible for thousands of square miles to be irrigated by the northern floodwaters without a drop of local rain. It could work for her given Luke's commitment to Winding River; he wouldn't leave now and put all his hard work in jeopardy.

A breathing space for them both?

Storm parked the Jeep at the rust-red base of the highest hill, picking her way carefully up the rocks to the flat-topped summit. A single ghost gum on top of it. She had a great view. Cattle were thundering towards the holding yards. Once Luke swooped so low her heart jumped into her mouth. What he could do with the helicopter was fantastic. Her father used to make the joke that Luke could lean out to open the gates of the holding yard without even landing, but Luke never did anything too risky. Apart from person safety, air regulations were too strict.

She watched for quite a while then when the helicopter swung inland, maybe to land, she began to pick her way downhill fossicking through the ancient stones. Little lizards were darting thither and yon but she took care not to touch them. The geckos if touched were so vulnerable their tails dropped off. A group of wild donkeys came to see what she was doing on their territory, but she shooed them off, hoping she wouldn't meet up with a feral camel. It was a station rule to refrain from shooting feral camels if possible but some of them were incredibly dangerous on their best days.

These hills and flat-topped mesas, so harsh and arid for most of the time, she'd seen them covered in the most beautiful delicate blooms after rain; wild hibiscus, morning glories, cleomes, lilac lamb's tails smothering the rough stones, the undulating waves of the green pussy tails massed to the far horizon. She was moving very carefully, for the hillside was covered in loose shale, when she spotted something glittering down below her, flashes of blue and green raised up along the serrated back of a chunk of rock. Opal?

She moved faster downhill, planting her feet firmly, treating the hill with respect, but to her horror her foot became snagged in the tangled old root of a spindly bush. She went hurtling like a train, trying desperately to retain her balance, her efforts undermined by the loose shale.

"Oh God!" she cried out, a sound that carried surprisingly far in the still desert air. She was sick with the fear of falling, smashing her face, her limbs into those rocks. It was a miracle she was staying on her feet. An instant after the thought she totally lost balance, ricked an ankle badly, before sliding helplessly down the slope....

She came to almost immediately she thought. Maybe a half a minute when she lost consciousness. She'd hit the back of her head on a half-submerged rock that had stopped her descent. She had blood on her hands. She'd thrown them out to protect her face. There was a powerful dull ache in her head. Storm could feel the lump without reaching back to touch it. But worse, far worse, she had sprained her ankle or... It was throbbing badly, swelling within her boot. Hell! She'd have to get herself out of this. The extraordinary part was for all the tumble her hat was still shoved down over her eyes. It might even have deadened the crack to her skull. Gingerly she went to sit up but as she did so her gaze fell on a snake in a defensive fanged position not four feet from her. A taipan, the largest and most feared venomous snake in the country, thus the world. Rich brown on top she could see its yellow and orange under spots. Its head was raised above its coiled body easily ten feet in length. It wasn't the first time she had encountered a snake, desert death adders, taipans. One lived with them in the interior but even the worst of them weren't aggressive unless threatened. Somehow that didn't give her a lot of heart.

There was no way she could move fast, not with her ankle. The snake could strike lightning fast if she startled it. What to do? She dared not throw anything. Instead of darting away it could attack. Between the throbbing in her ankle, her head, plus the glittering heat she wasn't thinking too clearly. In fact she felt woozy. She could stay perfectly still and the snake might lose interest and slither away. She thought it looked less alert. The head had lowered fractionally. They had antivenom on the station. That's if anyone would get to her in time. Storm held herself rigid scarcely daring to breathe. Go away, snake. Go away and find yourself some other little reptile to eat.

It seemed like an eternity until the taipan slid off disappearing into the sparse vegetation the same colour as itself. Just as well it hadn't been a dingo attracted by her blood. Very determinedly Storm began to move. Her akubra was protecting her face but the sun was scorching her arms and legs. If only she could discard that boot! Her foot was swelling so much the boot could hardly contain it.

Where was Luke? He had always found her as a child. But then it had always been Luke who had gone looking. She even remembered what he used to call her, little champ! She'd like that. Little champ. One of the boys. She'd have to be a champ now to get down the hill....

Luke!

He waved to the men as he took the chopper back up. He'd spotted the Jeep from the air and realised it was Storm. She'd always enjoyed watching the aerial muster, but she'd chosen a damned hot spot to do it not that there was a cool place away from the curving tranquil banks of a billabong. The strangest thing was he thought he'd heard her call his name.

Luke!

That was crazy, but he'd heard it. Now he had a strong urge to find out if she was okay. Probably she was fossicking around looking for white and crystal quartz, the sparkling stones polished by wind-blown sand until they resembled glossy gemstones. The Jeep he'd sighted far off was empty. He saw her at the same time. Her yellow hat and her yellow T-shirt were a blaze of colour against the rust-red rocks. He knew instantly there was something wrong. She appeared to be inching herself down the incline lying almost prone, but she raised her arm to wave to him.

Little champ!

Now why did he think of that? Their shared childhood of course. What a rebel she'd been! Always defying her father's overly strict edicts, always trailing after them like a little scout. In retrospect the Major had treated her more

like a precious porcelain doll than a living child full of
courage and high spirits. Maybe the fact the Major had
lost his young wife so tragically explained his overzealous
sense of protectiveness.

He put the chopper down at enough distance to prevent
the whirling rotors from showering her in sand. His mind
was racing, trying to fathom what had happened. He suspected she had lost her footing on the loose shale and taken
a tumble. Obviously she had injured either her foot or her
leg.

He took the slope with a mixture of speed and caution,
reaching her in the shortest possible time. He dropped to
his haunches staring down at her with a face taut with
anxiety.

"Where does it hurt?" Even as he spoke his eyes were
running over her. He saw the blood, he saw the grazes.
Her face was unmarked but she held her head gingerly. So
far as he could make out, the worst problem was her left
ankle. He would have to cut off the boot to release her
swollen foot.

"I hope—I think, it's sprained." She spoke calmly
enough, but she couldn't stop herself from gasping in pain.
"I hit my head, too. I'm sure there's a great lump. And a
bloody great snake," she gritted, "a taipan, kept me company for God knows how long before it decided to take
off."

He listened in horror, opening out the sharp blade of his
pocket-knife. "I'll be as gentle as I can."

"You'd better be," she said, but smiled.

As it was, she fainted while he swore softly in distress.
He removed the damaged boot very slowly. It was ruined.
The foot was very swollen. He didn't know yet whether it
was a bad sprain or she'd broken it. He prayed the former
though bad sprains caused the more pain. Sometimes, too,

a clean break was quicker to heal than torn ligaments. She was coming around, moaning a little. "It's all right, Storm." He bent to comfort her, stroking her cheek. "I'm here."

She murmured something, her face ashen. He looked back down the slope trying to gauge the best route to take. He settled on the way through the clumps of spinifex that dotted the cratered terrain. The spinifex would hold the soil and the stones there were larger, flatter, like pieces of sculpture. He would have to carry her so he could take no risks. He walked his proposed route first, pitching away the loose stones that mantled the ground, leaving his footprints as a track to follow.

"I'm sorry, Luke," she gasped as he lifted her into his arms. "I'm sorry...sorry..." Sorry for everything.

Storm spent two days in Base Hospital where Luke had made the decision to take her immediately after the accident. Her ankle was X-rayed. It proved not to be broken but sprained. With her youth and excellent state of fitness, it was anticipated she would make a trouble-free early recovery. The blow to her head was treated with caution. When she arrived at the hospital she was found to be concussed, so she was admitted for observation and her cuts and grazes cleaned up.

In the afternoon of the second day Luke came for her, landing the helicopter on the pad to the rear of the hospital. He found her inside the foyer waiting for him. They had her in a wheelchair and the sight smote him.

"Hi, how's it going?" He bent to kiss her pale cheek, his heart exposing him as a man deeply in love.

"Fine. I bet you're mad at me?" Tears of weakness shone in her beautiful green eyes.

"Can't you feel it?" He gave her his melting smile,

remembering the very many times she had said that to him in their lives. "In much pain?" He knew she wouldn't acknowledge it.

"I'm okay. One of the nurses lent me a dress. It's easy, button through."

"That was nice of her." The dress was loose like a child's smock, made of some light flowery material. She looked beautiful whatever she wore. "And the headaches?"

"They're all but gone, Doctor."

"Which reminds me I'd better have a word with him," Luke said, turning his head to look around.

"He left, Luke. He's gone with Sister Maree. There's been an accident on Mingari. One of the stockmen, I think."

"Too bad. Now let's get you out of here. I'll need a wards man to help me get you into the chopper but I shouldn't have any trouble getting you out."

Which was the case when they set down lightly as a bird on the homestead's huge circular drive.

"Just let yourself come down to me," he urged, holding up his arms.

She felt such pain in her ankle, she shut her eyes as he gathered her body to him, holding her closely, strongly, as if she were as insubstantial as a five-year-old.

Her silky black mane brushed his cheek. Magic. Crushing him beneath a weight of desire. "Put your arms around my neck," he advised, his voice so gentle and soothing she felt like a filly he was breaking in.

"What would I do without you," she exclaimed. It was meant as a truce, a peace offering but somehow, maybe because of the pain, it came out edgy.

"I'm sure you'll find out," he said, his sensitive antennae out.

Inside the house he set her down on a sofa in the drawing room. "Okay?" He had never seen her so pale.

She looked up at him, so vibrant with life. "Thank you, Luke. If you could get the crutches out of the chopper I should be able to manage on my own."

"Not today anyway. I've contacted Noni. Told her about your accident. She wants to come home."

"Oh, that's a shame! It means she won't be able to enjoy a longer stay with her friend."

"Don't worry about that," he said. "She *wants* to come, Storm. Besides you need someone. I'm sure you don't want me to help you dress and undress?" He had an irresistible vision of her slender naked body.

Her face lit up with a wry smile. "I know you'd do a good job. I've put everyone out haven't I? This is such a very busy time for you." She smoothed the full skirt of her borrowed dress then she lifted her eyes to him. "You *are* going to stay?"

His expression gave nothing away. "I won't leave you when you're like this, Storm. I won't leave until the big muster is over. I owe that to your father."

"Not to me?" She looked searchingly into his handsome, familiar face.

"I quit before I let you ask for my resignation." He said it like a joke but she knew it was no joke.

"I suppose I deserve that?"

"Maybe, but all this can wait, at least for the time being. The both of us have enough on our plate."

"I know," she sighed, "but we have to discuss it sometime."

"I think I'll wait until you've got some colour in your cheeks," he answered dryly, beginning to turn about. "I'll make some tea. You put your foot up." He found a cushion and placed it. "How long does the doctor think?"

"Two, three weeks." She winced a little as her foot came to rest, an involuntary movement of her facial muscles. "I'll see how I go."

"You'd be best advised to do as the doctor says," he warned, knowing Storm. "Ice packs, I suppose?"

"Yes. Don't worry about me, Luke," she said in a conciliatory voice. "This is nothing. Just a minor setback. When's Noni coming home?"

He paused at the door. "We can't expect her until the day after tomorrow. She'll come in with the freight plane." His eyes moved over her as she lay on the couch. "I'll stay here at the homestead tonight so you can sleep easy."

She wanted nothing more. Nothing more than he should touch her. Love her.

"The things you do for me," she said.

Luke didn't return to the house until well after seven. Hours lost were hours that had to be made up. He had showered and changed, the dark flame of his hair temporarily subdued by damp. He found her in the kitchen, crutches beneath her arms, going from the counter to the table.

"Here, let me do that." He crossed the large room in a couple of strides.

She surrendered without a fight. "I never knew how difficult it is to get around on crutches. I guess I'll learn."

Concern touched his eyes. "I told you I'd attend to all this, Storm. You know you should be off that foot as much as possible. Hopping around will only slow progress. I'm sorry, I'm so late. It was unavoidable."

"No apologies, Luke." She gave him a grateful look. "Thank you for taking the time."

"So what's on the menu?" He looked to see what she had managed so far.

"Salad as an entrée, salad for mains, salad for dessert,"

she joked. "That's as far as I got." She sank into a chair, letting Luke take the crutches from her, then she sat forward to rest her elbows on the table. She had covered it with a pale blue damask cloth that shone in the light. "There's a ham in the fridge, fillet steaks. I managed to thaw some smoked salmon. Take your pick."

"If it's okay with you I think I'll go for the steaks." He was hungry.

"Of course. A man needs filling. I'll stick to the salad and maybe a couple of slices of the salmon. I haven't been doing anything so I'm not terribly hungry. How's the muster progressing?"

"Right on schedule." He dipped into the refrigerator and withdrew a couple of steaks. "When you're properly on your feet again I'd like to show you how things are run. You're a good businesswoman, you'll take it all in your stride."

Storm was briefly quiet. "No Dad to contend with?"

"The Major was one of the old school. There are many, many things you need to know."

"And you're going to teach me?" She stared into his handsome face.

"I'm assuming you want to learn?"

"Of course I do." The black wings of her brows furrowed. "And what better teacher?"

He ignored that although it wasn't said provocatively. "Like a glass of wine?"

"Sure." A thirst rose in her throat. "You'll have to go down to the cellar. I wasn't up to those stairs."

"Mind a red?" He paused at the cellar door. "No time to chill a white."

"Red will be fine. A good Shiraz."

He was back within moments, going to a drawer for the corkscrew. It came to her that she loved watching him move about. He had such method about him, a clear, cool, logical mind. No unnecessary shuttling. Economy of movement. It made her smile.

Over the meal he began to talk to her about the McFarlane operation, which was far more involved than she had imagined. She, in turn, spoke about her father's extensive portfolio, which she had inherited, not terribly surprised when it appeared he already knew pretty much the extent of it. Not that he claimed prior knowledge but it was evident to her her father had taken Luke into his confidence. In fact Luke raised suggestions, showing his own knowledge of the share market and how to play it. He even suggested a different broker, citing a name. "They're more on the ball than the crowd your father had been dealing with for years. You need new blood."

The conversation continued at an engrossed pace even after they moved to more comfortable chairs in the sunroom. Both were in accord, Luke seemed relaxed. What better time to approach the dilemma that lay between them and try to resolve it, Storm thought, deliberately introducing the subject. "You said once you wanted to start your own operation."

A small shrug though his body tensed. "Even your father knew that, Storm. I owed him so much. He gave me a home, a first-class education, even the damned clothes I stood up in until I could finally earn. But I made no secret of the fact I always wanted to be my own man."

"Dad would have admired that."

"It was scarcely why I did it."

"I know. I don't want to force you to reject your share of Winding River, Luke. It was Dad's wish that you have it. I promise you I won't go against his wishes. I have no thought in my mind of contesting the will."

"Why not?" He gazed at her with his intensely blue

eyes. "You'd probably win. Bring in the big guns. The thing is, Storm, it's too massive a bequest. Not easy to accept. Not easy for you."

She took a breath. "Dad wouldn't have been around if you hadn't saved his life?"

"Maybe that was exaggerated." He brushed the idea off.

"I don't think so. Dad himself said he thought he was done for. I won't fight your share, Luke. As far as I'm concerned you're entitled to the profits as well. You'd be working the whole operation."

A range of warring emotions crossed his face. "You know what your father had in mind?"

She nodded her dark head. "Pretty feudal wasn't he? He was practically *giving* me away."

Luke's shapely mouth set. "He thought it would work. An arranged marriage no less."

"Just like the good old days," she crowed. "So what would have happened had I married Alex or someone like him and you married Carla or her successor? Didn't he think it through?"

Luke answered, almost angrily. "Obviously not. You knew your father, Storm. What he wanted *had* to be. Of course as a business arrangement it would have worked fine."

She considered that, unnerved. "You mean you'd accept your inheritance if I consented to marry you?"

He studied her with his blue level gaze. Somehow she had changed out of the borrowed dress. She was wearing a little violet singlet top that showed off the beautiful neat shape of her breasts, with a sarong splashed with fuchsia and violet flowers, wrapped around her slender hips. It was as if he'd always known these hungers for her, yet answered crisply. "I don't mean that at all. When I get married, Storm, it'll be because I can't live without that one woman in my life, and she can't live without *me*.''

At the look in his eyes her cheeks flamed and she dropped her gaze. ''Are you telling me you haven't met her?'' She cursed herself for being such an emotional coward.

''Oh I've met her all right,'' he clipped off, ''but she's all locked away behind emotional barriers.''

''Not of her own making...you know they weren't *all* self-inflicted...''

''Maybe not,'' he sighed, ''but she's the only person in the world who can knock them down.''

He carried her up to her room. They could have taken the lift that had been installed a few years back when the Major was having difficulty with the grand staircase, but there was too much pleasure in having her in his arms, no matter the inevitable torment.

''So what are you going to sleep in?'' he asked after he set her down on the huge, canopied bed. Such a beautiful bedroom she had, fit for a princess.

''This will do.'' She glanced down at herself, not wanting to go to the least bit of bother. The briefs she was wearing matched the singlet. The sarong was simple to untie. ''I'll splash my face and clean my teeth.''

''I'll go get your crutches,'' he said. ''Turn off the lights.''

She didn't even wait, hopping the short distance into the *en suite*, grabbing onto the porcelain basin for support, her left leg bent up at the knee. By the time he returned she was hopping back to the bed.

''God there's no stopping you, is there?'' he said, torn between amusement and dismay.

"I managed okay. The trick is to not put your injured foot to the ground."

"You will try to remember what I told you about making good progress?"

"Yes, brother, dear."

"Cut it out."

She felt a jolt. "I'm sorry."

"You're a cruel little cat," he said quietly.

"But I meant it sincerely. I am sorry. You know as well as I do my tongue always runs away with me."

"You don't have to let it. Are you sure there's nothing else I can get you? You might need painkillers during the night?"

"Then I'll call out to you," she said sweetly, putting her hands behind her head and making a plait.

"You'd better not," he warned.

"Why, what might happen?" she asked softly, her green eyes glowing.

His answer was curt. "What's going to happen if I don't get out of this room."

"So I'm sexually satisfactory at least." Something was pushing her into being provocative. Blind *need?*

"Good night, Storm," he said without a smile, turning on his heel.

"Good night, Luke. Aren't you going to kiss me before you go?"

"You're a mystery to me, Storm. That much I know."

"A woman should always be a mystery to her man," she came back at him.

"You're taking it for granted, aren't you, I'm *your* property?"

"Why not?" she said discordantly. "I'm yours. If you wanted to you could carry me off."

"As what, first prize?"

She threw herself backwards across the bed, her eyes filling with tears at the faint lash in his voice. "Don't go, Luke."

He groaned in frustration, struggling under the weight of pride and his pent-up desires, knowing himself trapped.

"Don't go," she whispered, turning her raven head that had already escaped its thick plait. Its silken coils swirled all over the pale gold brocade of the quilt. "Share my bed with me. Share Winding River." She extended one slender arm. "The way things are, there's no escape."

He agreed. How could he not? But the years of duelling had to cease. He wanted liberation. For himself. More importantly for her. Looking at her lying across the bed like that, his strong desires broke their leash. Impetuously he crossed to her bed, positioning himself directly behind her head, then he dropped to his knees, cupping the lovely alluring oval of her face between his hands. Storm, his heart's desire. "Witch!" he murmured, kissing her glowing eyes shut.

"All witches have green eyes." She flung back her arms, digging her fingers into the fiery thickness of his hair. "Kiss me until you can kiss me no more."

For the briefest moment he considered drawing away, a gesture meant to torment her as she had tormented him for years, but her pulsing mouth was just beneath his. "Have you thought I could hurt you," he muttered, "knock your ankle?" It was a genuine concern.

"I don't care." She looked into his marvellous face, the risk of some pain to her ankle counterbalanced by the anticipation of the priceless pleasure only he could give her. "I can't promise I won't scream." She gave him a slow, tantalising smile.

"Then I'll have to be very, very gentle."

In one exquisitely controlled movement he rolled the

violet singlet off her, slipping it over her head. "You're so beautiful!" Her skin gave off such a lustre in the light. Like ivory satin. "*So* beautiful," he repeated, laying his head between her breasts, inhaling the seductive scents of her woman's body. "I can hear your heart pumping," he murmured, revelling in her heart-breaking, open-mouthed sighs of rapture.

"It beats for you," she whispered, never once looking away from his eyes. So then, very slowly, Luke moved onto the bed beside her, careful where he was placing his long, lean body, feeling the huge bed take his weight. Such intimacy he had only dreamed of! He pressed his mouth to the blue pulse that beat so wildly, betrayingly in her throat.

CHAPTER EIGHT

LUKE had just finished talking to the station's resident saddler when he spotted the light aircraft coming in from the north east. A few minutes more and he could confirm his educated guess: a single engine Piper. It could only be one person. Carla. Her father had bought it for her a few years back. No toy, but the vehicle best suited their unique way of life. He knew what Carla wanted. She wanted to check out what was happening on Winding River. It was no secret Noni had taken leave. That left him and Storm alone. In that extraordinary way women have, Carla had long divined his heart despite all the dramas and clashes between him and Storm. Carla had seen straight into the secret places, though he had never discussed Storm with her at any time, nor had he ever risen to the barbed remarks Carla had thrown his way.

He had stopped his relationship with Carla almost at the time Storm had broken off her engagement to Alex. Carla had taken it better than he hoped, making him promise they would always remain friends. He thought that was so. Carla always appeared to have accepted the shift in the relationship. It struck him unpleasantly from time to time that Carla had instigated a few breaks of her own with a couple of his former girlfriends. Carla had always been ready to sew disinformation, even downright lies, always denying them convincingly when questioned. Scheming he had come to see was at the centre of Carla's being. Outside of that when she got what she wanted, she was good company. But his feelings for her had never amounted to being in love even if their relationship had transcended the merely sexual.

Now he saw he had trouble. Carla was another one who believed she could never lose.

He arrived at the airstrip moments before she set down, waiting for her to complete her after checks.

"Luke, how's it going?" She rushed to him, her attractive face lit up in a bright smile, that in no way reflected her central tensions. "I heard on the grape vine about Storm's accident. With Noni being away I thought I'd do the neighbourly thing and volunteer my services. It can't be easy for her until her ankle heals."

What was he supposed to do? Give her coffee and send her on her way. Storm wouldn't be agreeable he knew. The two were not close.

"That's kind of you, Carla," he said, unwilling to hurt her by refusing her quick kiss. "I suppose you got your information from the hospital?"

"As a matter of fact, yes. One of our stockmen broke a few ribs and his collarbone. A bullock pinned him between a gate and the fence."

"He's okay?"

"He'll live," she said cheerily. "How is it up at the house? Pretty dismal I should think. Storm adored her father."

"Yes, she did," he answered quietly.

"Not that she was the best daughter in the world to him." Carla gave him a quick you'd-have-to-agree-with-me glance.

Instead he retorted. "What's that supposed to mean?"

She reached up to pat his shoulder. "Now, now, don't get hot under the collar about your pal, Storm. Honestly, the way you two grew up! It was damned near incestuous." She gave a little laugh.

"It was damned near nothing of the kind," Luke responded in a voice that should have warned Carla off. "I hope you don't go around repeating that sort of thing?" He could well believe that she might.

"Sweetie." Carla was all innocence. "A lot of people think so. The Major treated you like his son and heir."

His strong jaw tightened. "The Major has gone now, Carla. I'd appreciate it if you don't stir things up and put our friendship at risk."

Her brown eyes, her best feature, shone with ready tears. "As if I'd ever do that." She began to walk towards the Jeep, speaking over her shoulder. "I expect the will has been read?"

"You surely don't think I'm about to discuss it with you, Carla?"

She scanned his taut, handsome face. "Knowing you, no. I'm sorry about what I said before," she apologised. "I know what Storm means to you. But even you can't deny she didn't visit her father as often as she could have."

"She rang him regularly," Luke said abruptly, looming over her. "She has a career, you know."

"Ah yes, the brilliant jewellery designer!" Carla exclaimed. "I expect if she hadn't sprained her ankle she'd be back in Sydney now?"

Luke recognised this couldn't go on. "Carla, what did you really come for," he asked quietly. "I'm not going to have you upsetting Storm. I somehow feel that's your aim."

A red flush whipped upwards from her throat. "What a terrible thing to say! Is that what you think of me, Luke?"

He looked over her head. "I can't help remembering some of the mischief you've made."

She struggled to deny it then realised it was impossible. "You know what they say? All's fair in love and war."

"That's all over, Carla." He regarded her with a mixture of sympathy and wariness. "I never led you to believe I was after a commitment."

"Of course you didn't." She tossed her head. "You laid it straight on the line. We were two adults in need of comfort. Speaking of comfort, Storm must be one of the richest women in the country?"

He tried to keep his cool but she was making him angry. "That's her business, Carla. She'll be very rich certainly."

"I just hope the Major left a sizeable legacy to you?" she asked him with considerable directness.

"Why do you say that?" he parried not about to take her into his confidence.

"Because he knew your worth," Carla almost jeered. "We all know Storm will head back to Sydney. Probably she'll sell up. She can't run the operation."

"You obviously don't know Storm," he said crisply. "She'll never sell Winding River. The McFarlanes pioneered this part of the world."

"So? Not all the old families are still around. It makes sense for her to sell it. I know Dad would jump at the chance to acquire it. The banks are lending again. If we sell off a few interests... This is one of the best operations in the country. In these last few years that's largely been due to you. We could make plans, Luke. You and I."

So she had never chosen to believe their relationship was over. "Carla, the last thing I want to do is hurt you," he said, his face set, "but there's no *we*. Stop knocking your head against a brick wall."

She looked up at him and put a finger to his lips. "Shh! It may appear like that to you, but to my way of thinking you're the one who's doing the head knocking. You just won't accept you'll never get Storm. She's way too big a prize. Even for you."

After last night that thought didn't strike him. "Carla, this conversation is getting downright depressing. Feeling like you do I think it's best if you fly off home. Our relationship failed, accept it once and for all. If we're going to pay attention to the grape vine, I've heard you and Les Marshall are pretty close."

She stiffened as though she'd be thrown off balance. "Les is just a playmate. Nothing serious. A woman likes to feel wanted."

"Men do, too," he said. "Listen, I can offer you a coffee."

She smiled. "That's nice of you, Luke, but I really did come to see Storm. You're making me out a bitch with an unpleasant taste for making trouble, but my motivation couldn't be purer. I want to be of help. I know Storm isn't a friendly person but Mum was on my back to come over. We really feel for Storm. Everyone does. Why can't you give me a bit of credit?"

"Maybe because I've learned my lesson," he said suavely.

She stood looking into his eyes. "For a sweet man you have a cruel streak. At least take me up to the house to say hello. I can see what Storm thinks. If she doesn't need a woman's help I swear I'm prepared to fly back home."

"Is that a promise?" he asked in a very wry tone.

"Trust me, Luke," she exclaimed, thinking if he did, he'd be dead wrong.

Storm heard Carla's voice before she saw her. She'd been sitting quietly in the sunroom, perfecting some of her blueprints for a new collection of jewellery when the sound of Carla's bright confident voice broke into her concentration.

Oh Lord, she thought, mourning the temporary loss of privacy. She and Carla had never been close. In fact they had seen little of each other over the years for all the two stations Winding River and Mingari bordered. They had gone to different boarding schools. Carla had not gone on to University preferring to come back to the Outback. Storm had forged a career in Sydney.

Then there was *Luke*. A state of affairs that now had a tremendous bearing on their never too friendly relationship.

A minute later and Carla all but bounded into the room, as eager and attractive as usual, dressed in a pink shirt and matching jeans that set off her tan. Luke was a few steps behind her, looking not altogether happy.

Briefly their eyes met.

"Storm!" Carla gave a little sympathetic cry and rushed forward to drop a peck on Storm's cheek. "Poor old you! We had news of your accident. Mum and I decided that the nice, neighbourly thing to do was for me to come over. You must be finding it difficult hopping about on crutches?" Her eyes went to the crutches Storm had placed beside her.

Storm felt quite unable to be ungracious. "That was kind of you, Carla. You flew yourself over?"

Carla nodded, looking towards Luke and smiling as though the three of them were the greatest of friends. "I came prepared to stay a few days. That's if you want me." There was a little catch in her voice as though being wanted was important to her.

It threw Storm slightly, making her revise her recent impressions of Carla. Still, she didn't want Carla's company. She had Luke. But how to convey that without hurt? "That'd be nice, Carla," she said injecting as much warmth as she could, "but Noni is coming home tomorrow."

A light flush swept Carla's face. "That's great! Good news. I knew she'd want to be with you. Until tomorrow then," she suggested, her gaze going back and forth, a little anxious. "Until Noni arrives. Mum and I felt sure you'd want another woman on hand."

Storm's mind filled with wry humour at that. "That was kind of you both to think of me, Carla, but I've been managing okay."

Carla's voice became more persuasive yet. "It's important you don't try to do too much, too early," she warned. "I know you'll be wanting to get back to Sydney as soon as you can. I see you're doing some sketches." Her inquisitive eyes flew to the table.

Storm nodded and gently closed the sketchpad. "A new collection. It's not really the time to be doing it but I made a commitment. I sell some of my jewellery through an art dealer who arranged a showing of my work with that of a simpatico artist. The combination worked well in the past."

"You're so clever," said Carla in an admiring undertone. "Please don't think I'm here to get in your way. I only want to be on hand should you need help."

Storm wondered how she could possibly get out of this short of rudeness. She didn't want that. "I do have Luke," she pointed out gently, allowing her gaze to settle on Luke's tall, rangy figure.

"Not *all* the time!" Carla protested, just barely keeping her feelings of outrage to herself, "besides we're all into the big muster, aren't we, Luke?" She looked to him for back-up.

"We're going well," Luke remarked so briefly, Carla pulled a face.

"Oh dear, it almost sounds like you don't want me to stay?" Her face fell visibly, the expression in her golden-brown eyes full of hurt.

Storm lacked the toughness to tell Carla to go, "Oh please, Carla," she said, "stay overnight by all means. It's a long way home."

Carla made a lightning recovery, turning to Luke with now dancing eyes. "I brought just one overnight bag with me. It's in the Jeep. I'll go with you and get it. Mum and I would hate to think we left Storm alone with her swollen ankle. Let alone her grief. Never underestimate the importance of friendship I say."

Despite her professed wish to be "on hand" for Storm, Carla spent several hours of the afternoon going in search of Luke before finally catching up with him at Cash's Crossing. This was a drafting camp near the river where branding, earmarking and other operations were being carried out. Calves and mothers in particular were always treated as gently as possible. Not only were the most humane methods in operation, gentle handling was a big asset to beef production for docility of temperament in cattle was an important factor in increased beef production. On no account was rough handling of the stock on Winding River permitted under punishment of "the sack."

Carla returned to the homestead towards sunset full of everything she had seen around the station; loudly applauding Luke for the many improvements he had made; how wonderfully *quiet* was the big muster.

"Dad always says the boss of any outfit has to have great people sense as well as great cattle sense. Luke is marvellously skilled at both. I know I shouldn't be asking this, Storm..."

So *don't,* Storm pleaded inwardly knowing if a question had to be so prefaced it was better left unasked.

"…but Luke tells me the Major's will has been read," Carla continued, eyeing Storm off. Storm felt a stab like betrayal then she reminded herself of Carla's devious nature. She kept silent, so Carla rushed on.

"Of course it was just in passing," Carla explained, "he didn't go out of his way to tell me or anything. Feeling about Luke as I do." She gave Storm a bright-eyed glance. "I just wondered if the Major had left him anything. I expect he did. The Major was such a wonderfully generous man. Luke is a living testament to that."

Count ten. Why ten? She asked herself. She really needed half an hour. "Surely if you discussed my father's will, you and Luke being so close, he would have told you?" Storm asked very coolly.

It didn't put Carla off, she shrugged. "You know Luke. He's a bit like the Major the way he keeps things to himself."

Storm considered. "My father did remember, Luke, Carla." Her tone she kept even. "I'd rather not discuss it however."

Carla's eyes lit with little golden flames. "Substantial, I would say, from the expression on your face. I know he'll get around to telling me. It's no secret Luke wants his own cattle run. He's a man who likes doing things his way."

It really was time to shift, if she could. Storm eyed her crutches. "I'm absolutely certain Luke and Dad saw eye-to-eye," she said.

"In most things I guess, but Luke did have concerns…" Again Carla left it up in the air; to be guessed at. "That's the difference between us, Storm," she pointed out kindly. "You never bothered your head about the McFarlane operation. I quite understand that. Your interests are artistic. In my own case, I wanted to know exactly how Mingari works. Dad sometimes says I know more about it than the boys.''

Storm didn't doubt it. The Prentice boys weren't overly bright. "I'm sure you'll be a great asset to your husband," Storm said. "Whether he's a cattleman or not. Just for the record, Carla, I always wanted to know about the station but Dad thought women and cattle operations didn't mix. I guess in many ways, however, as much I loved him, he was the ultimate chauvinist.''

Carla gave her a shocked look, then a faint smile. "What a thing to say about your father.''

"Dad wouldn't have minded." Storm shrugged. "He was the first to recognise that quality in himself only he thought it was greatly to be desired.''

"You *do* have a sharp tongue." Carla's tone was censorious.

"I like to tell the truth, yes." Storm moved restlessly, causing Carla to jump up.

"Now what are we going to have for dinner tonight?" she asked in very bright tones. "I'm not quite as good as Noni but pretty close. Mum always saw to it I knew my way around a kitchen. We never had a live-in housekeeper and cook like you." She gave Storm a look that set Storm's teeth together.

"Noni's *family,* Carla, not just an employee. Many's the time I've cried on Noni's shoulder.''

"You have?" Carla looked amazed. "I can't imagine you crying, Storm. You always seem so self-contained. We were all amazed how composed you were at the funeral. I found it so hard...now I thought we might ask Luke up for dinner? Does that suit you?''

Storm had the sense of brushing up against a steamroller. "Carla, I couldn't have stopped you asking if I tried."

Carla hadn't been exaggerating when she said she was a good cook. In fact she had pulled out all the stops over dinner, turning it into a gala occasion when it was only a handful of days since she had attended Athol McFarlane's funeral and found it very hard. Surely not the most sensitive woman in the world, Storm thought, and this is not to impress me. She was impressed all the same.

"Where did you find all this?" she had to ask, unaware there was so much produce at hand.

"You'd be amazed at what you have in the cold room." Carla looked smug. "Noni has stocked up on just about everything you can think of. The little pasta entrée was very easy. I'll be happy to give you the recipe. I know Luke loves pasta. The aged beef was to hand. All I've added is a grilled vegetable salad with anchovy butter."

"I wish I were more hungry to do it justice," Storm said without malice. "I'm not the country's most brilliant cook."

Carla's reply was instantaneous. "I'd be glad to give you a few lessons. You don't have to ask Luke if he's hungry!" she added, looking at Luke's near empty plate with satisfaction. She touched him affectionately on the hand. "There's lots more."

"All in good time, Carla," Luke said smoothly.

"You're going to love dessert."

"There's more?" Storm concentrated hard on not groaning.

"I have to remind you, Storm, the way to a man's heart is through his stomach."

"Maybe that's just an old wives' tale," Storm said.

"My dear Storm, but it *is*. Mum says it's absolutely critical a woman knows how to cook."

"It would seem so. This *is* turning into a banquet."

Carla started to laugh. "Come on, this is a nice meal. Remember the reason I'm here. I want to look after you." She turned her head to Luke. "I think you're going to love my peppered pineapple with vanilla coconut ice cream. It might sound funny but it's delicious."

"Carla," said Luke, "your mother must be very proud of you."

Afterwards they had coffee out on the verandah, the black velvet sky incandescent with stars. The evening had gradually merged into Carla's telling one preposterous story after another, but Storm had to admit quite a few of them were funny. Carla liked to act out the various parts, changing her voice frequently to suit the character. She was an excellent mimic, leading Storm to remark she would have made a good actress.

Carla looked at Storm quickly to see if she was joking, which she wasn't. "For God's sake, Storm," she burst out, "the very last thing I'd want is to strut my stuff on a stage."

Luke lifted his head a fraction from the back of the chair to say, "You don't have to relinquish the idea, Carla. All the world's a stage according to our friend, Shakespeare."

"But darling." Carla touched him lightly on the arm. She was always touching him: his shoulder, his hand, his arm, his cheek. "There's nothing more I want than to be a good station wife."

"And mother of a brood, I hope?" Storm broke in. "Being the only one isn't a great blessing."

"Well, you would know," Carla laughed. In reality she was quite miffed at Storm's exotic appearance. It just had to be for dramatic effect to put her in the shade. From

somewhere Storm had got hold of an Indian sari, glowing
emerald in colour, printed with gold medallions with a
wide gold border. She had draped it around herself in a
surprisingly expert fashion, Carla thought. I mean how
many times had Storm worn a sari? Yet tonight she looked
like a young maharanee or something with that mane of
raven hair and those cat's eyes that echoed the colour of
the sari. It was all so threatening Carla thought. No one
should be that beautiful. The sooner Storm was back where
she belonged the better!

Storm, not entirely unaware of the trend of Carla's
thought, leant back in her peacock chair, her injured foot
resting on a cushioned footstool. For a while now she had
been pretending to listen to Carla while taking the opportunity to study Luke's striking face as familiar as her own,
yet she never tired of looking at it. He had such a beautiful
mouth. A sensual mouth. It had left its imprint on her. It
had left its imprint on Carla. Small wonder Carla still
wanted him. Certainly that was why Carla was here. Not
to be on hand for her. To be near Luke. To impress on
him she was the kind of wife he needed. Luke's breaking
off the relationship with Carla had only strengthened
Carla's resolve. Love affairs were sad, Storm thought.
Someone had to lose. And so she felt pity for Carla who
despite her determined camaraderie had no love in her
heart for Storm. In fact she was coming close to hating
her.

By ten o'clock Storm was tiring of what struck her as
an incongruous *ménage à trois*. As the evening wore on
Carla adopted an increasingly proprietorial attitude towards Luke, her manner intent on conveying to Storm their
brief affair was far from finished. Luke countered with a
few sardonic remarks that should have urged her to change
tack, but Carla chose to ignore them.

"What about a walk?" she suggested, as though the evening's entertainment wasn't over. She looked towards Luke, pressing his arm. "We won't leave Storm long. Just a quick stroll."

"Don't feel bad about it," Storm said, when Carla was looking anything but glum. "I feel a little tired anyway. I'll say good-night. Many thanks for cooking dinner, Carla. It was excellent."

"Why you hardly touched a bite!" Carla exclaimed. "I'll help you upstairs. We can take the lift. What a help to have it in the house like this."

Luke side-stepped Carla's suggestion. "It's okay. I'll carry her." He stood up, as superbly fit as a man could be. "Straight up the staircase, along the hall. I don't like to see you struggling with those crutches."

"Hey, I thought I was getting good."

"She *is* good," Carla maintained stoutly, in no mood to see Storm in Luke's arms.

"Not good enough for me." Luke shifted his chair out of the way, then moved over to the peacock chair where Storm reclined. "Ready?"

"My hero!" Storm sighed lightly.

Carla didn't like that. She didn't like it at all. Worse, she found she couldn't bear to see Luke cradling Storm in his arms. Something about the attitude of their bodies deeply disturbed her. They looked so comfortable together. No, comfortable wasn't the word, though Storm's body accommodated itself easily to Luke's. They looked like…primitive emotions surfaced…they looked like *lovers*. There wasn't the tiniest doubt in her mind. Oh God, Carla thought. They've slept together. Their body language said it all.

"I'll tend to the dishes," Carla called, watching Luke carry Storm up the grand central staircase. Why didn't he

drop her, Carla thought, instead of doing a Rhett Butler.
Before she could stop herself she made a bee-line to the
rear staircase, which gave onto the upper gallery. From
there she swept out onto the verandah inching down to
Storm's bedroom, as though there might be an orgy in
progress. She was taking a risk, she knew. Luke might
walk out onto the verandah, but she thought not. The
French doors and the wooden shutters were fastened back.
And there was cover. Golden canes in big glazed pots were
set at intervals all along the verandah, their billowing
fronds providing shelter.

For years, and no exaggeration, she had done everything
in her power to make Luke Branagan notice her. Finally
she had succeeded though her strategies, frenetic as they
were, hadn't been good enough to hold him. She had always known about the strong bond between Luke and
Storm but that had been kept in balance by endless con-
flicts. Now this! How and when had it happened? When
had the gulf been bridged?

By the Major's will? Luke had been named as a major
beneficiary. That was a little difficult to swallow. Storm
would be mad and she didn't seem mad at all. Determined
to know, no matter the cost, Carla stole along to the bedroom, positioning herself stealthily beside one of the
golden canes that flanged the bedroom door. Jealousy was
slicing through her with the sharpness of a blade. She felt
a twisted sense of betrayal. Didn't Storm McFarlane have
enough without taking Luke? She was a witch. There were
a few still around. One of those dark-haired, green-eyed
women that cast spells. Storm didn't want Luke. They'd
been combatants for years. She just wanted to show her
power. She could hear them talking inside the bedroom,
their voices low.

"I think Carla knows," Storm was saying, sounding like she was dismayed.

"Knows?" That was Luke. "You mean about us? It wouldn't surprise me. Carla's very sharp. I suppose it's all spelled out the way I look at you."

Carla heard the sigh. I don't want your pity, Storm McFarlane, she thought. I want you to disappear to Sydney and never come back.

Then Luke spoke and Carla sobered enough to listen. "I'm afraid you're right," he said. "But Carla has to face facts. Noni will be here tomorrow. Carla will be free to go home."

So he can't wait to get rid of me, Carla seethed. Off with the old and on with the new.

"I think Carla thinks her dislike of me is going unnoticed," Storm said in her cut-glass voice.

"Well it's not going unnoticed by *me*." Luke's attractive tones slightly hardened. "There are two sides to Carla," he added thoughtfully. "She could make a good enemy."

Too right I can! Carla thought, her passion for Luke dissolving into a fuming rage.

"Then be careful when you go for a walk with her." Storm gave a little laugh.

Carla thought Luke would answer, but there was silence. A silence that stretched unbearably. Overwhelmed with jealousy Carla peered around the shutters only to see Luke bending over Storm, seated on the bed. They were kissing.

And such kissing! Carla felt the hot blood rush to her cheeks. He had never kissed her like that. Those were light-hearted pecks compared to what she was seeing now. This was a grand passion. She wasn't such a fool she couldn't interpret that. Why was she worrying about being seen? If she beat a drum they wouldn't even hear her.

Carla turned on her heel and fled the way she had come. Still full of vain hopes. Still full of plans...

Noni arrived home midmorning, surprised to find Carla had come to visit, but encouraged by the pleasantness of Carla's manner, her competence and her regard for Storm's well-being. Carla seemed so genuinely friendly, Noni, who had never really taken to her before now, revised her opinion.

It was Carla who thoughtfully made morning tea and served it in the sunroom. Afterwards, she excused herself so Storm and Noni could have a private talk. There were many things Storm wouldn't say to her, Carla had decided, but she would confide in Noni, loyal family friend and retainer. When that happened Carla proposed to be somewhere within earshot. She felt not the slightest shame at the thought of eavesdropping. Sometimes it was the only way one could flush out confidential information.

In the end it took an interminable half an hour for Storm to bring up the subject of her father's will, a half hour during which Carla was supposed to be packing her overnight bag and putting the guest bedroom to rights. Carla, however, had taken up a position on a lower step of the rear staircase, cramming her ears to hear what was being said in the sunroom.

There was the whole tiresome episode of Storm's accident. Who hadn't been confronted by a snake? Carla thought and almost groaned. General talk about people Carla didn't even know, then just when Carla was about to give up and go upstairs Storm began to tell Noni the terms of her father's will.

Bingo! Carla kissed her fingers.

Starting with the bequest to Noni herself. Far too generous for a servant, Carla thought, barely controlling a sniff.

Then the bombshell! The unexpectedness of which had Carla on her feet, tiptoeing closer to the door. Luke had inherited a half share of Winding River. Something called life estate. Not only that, before Carla could even catch her breath, the news he would take the profits providing he continued to work the whole operation. It came like a blow that almost knocked Carla out. In one stroke, Athol McFarlane had made Luke a rich man, a real player. Whatever else she had imagined, a splendid lump sum, she had never for one moment anticipated Luke would be given equal share with the Major's only daughter. Her immediate thought was, it was unfair. So the Major had doted on Luke almost like a son? Luke wasn't his blood.

There was absolutely no way Noni expected it, either.

"But darling girl how extraordinary!" she cried. "It seems a great deal for *affection,* though I know no one has worked harder than Luke. He certainly deserved recognition, but this, it quite takes my breath away."

My sentiments exactly, thought Carla, continuing her detective work.

"Dad had plans, Noni," Storm explained. "I think his dearest wish was to see Luke and I married."

Tears of outrage came to Carla's eyes.

"Luke would keep the station going. I would provide the heirs."

Silence again. Carla pictured them side by side. "But how do you feel about this, dearest girl?" Noni still sounded like a woman in shock. "How does Luke? I know it would have come as a great surprise to him."

Surprise. *Indeed!* Carla fumed.

"It did. To us both," Storm said. "I'm afraid I reacted so badly, Luke threatened to leave. He said he wanted no part of any legacy. He wouldn't work for me—'' Storm broke off, thinking she heard a small sound. "Was that something?"

Carla waited for no more. As if she had taken wings she swooped up the stairs making for the guest room. She accomplished it with such quietness and such speed by the time Noni came to the door of the sunroom to investigate, the rear hall and the surrounding area, were quite empty.

"Nothing, darling," Noni said reassuringly. "Nothing at all."

It seemed graceless in the extreme to send Carla off without lunch so after unpacking her things and settling in, Noni returned to her domain, pleased to find it spotless, to organize lunch. Her mind was still trying to cope with Storm's news; the fact Luke had inherited half share in Winding River had put her own sizeable legacy on the backburner. Luke was a truly exceptional young man. She really cared about him. It was Noni's own view that he would make a fine husband for her beloved Storm. The more she thought about it, marrying would seem to solve the problem. At the same time it could have thrown them into a new dilemma. What a master manipulator the Major had been, God rest his soul. Noni went out to her vegetable garden to find the making for a salad.

Meanwhile on the front verandah Storm and Carla made casual conversation, Storm trying her hardest to be friendly for all she found it a little heavy going. Carla, waited her moment. Then let the chips fall where they may! Finally it came. Storm passed some remark about Luke's having to visit the outstations, giving Carla the opportunity to insert gently, sounding troubled, "It must have come as an awful shock Luke inheriting half of Winding River?" She looked at Storm, her eyes full of sympathy. "I know in your place I would be devastated."

Storm could hear Carla's words, but they seemed to be coming from a long way off. In fact it was difficult to describe the full impact Carla's words had on her. Anger uppermost. A horrendous pain like a stab to the heart. "Wherever did you get that information from, Carla?" She stared at her, not believing it could have come from Luke. Not Luke! Not now she had delivered herself up to him.

"Why, Luke, of course," Carla confessed, sounding a little frightened. "He told me when we went for a walk last night. Please don't tell him I told you," she begged. "He'd be very angry with me. It was supposed to be a secret to share."

Was it possible she was telling the truth? Storm thought grimly. A lie could easily be found out. "What else did he tell you?" Storm asked.

"Oh, Storm, I'm sorry." Carla put her hand to her burning face. "I should never have said anything but I thought we were friends. It was the last thing I expected to hear. Luke told me it was only for his lifetime. He did explain that. That helped a bit. The station will revert to you. As it *should*."

"And Luke told you all this last night?" Storm asked, aware her tones were very blunt.

Carla hung her head. "I can see I've made you very angry. But, Storm, my sympathies are with *you*. Why if Dad did that to me…" She gestured helplessly.

Her whole heart wanted to believe in Luke but this smacked of the truth. Where else would Carla have got it from?

"Regardless of whether Luke is angry with you or not, Carla, I intend to speak to him about this."

"And ruin my chances with him?" Carla's eyes filled with tears. "Storm you can't be so cruel. I love Luke."

"Then I'm very sorry for you, Carla. He doesn't love you."

There was a look of total denial in Carla's eyes. "Maybe not now but he *will* in time. There's no life for him with you, Storm. For any number of reasons. You're always looking down your nose at him. He *hates* that. He hates the way you've always played the lovely lady of the manor."

"Did he tell you that?" Storm's voice suggested she was highly sceptical.

"Storm, surely you know Luke and I have spent a lot of time together. You were off in Sydney most of the time. You got yourself engaged twice. Luke had to have someone to confide in. Is it so hard to believe he'd confide in me?"

That seemed to echo endlessly in Storm's head. "I suppose not," she said eventually. "And how would the fact Luke has inherited half share in Winding River affect you? I've told you, you've lost any hold over Luke."

"That's not what I sense when I'm alone with him. He trusts me unlike you. Anyway, surely he can sell out to you?" Carla's trim body was taut with excitement.

"Did he say that?" Storm's brain was spinning.

"Luke is a man who considers his options," Carla said, respectfully. "I know his first thought was simply to go. He's a proud man. But I suppose you convinced him not to leave you in the lurch. I wouldn't want that either. You'll go back to your career, Storm. We all know that. You get your face in all the glossy magazines. All the time. I know you're not a social butterfly, or anything like that, but you *are* social. It occurs to me you could even sell to Luke?"

She'd come this far she might as well go on. "How would Luke come by the money?" Storm asked.

Carla's triumphant expression shaped itself into careful consideration as though this were a question intended to be taken very seriously. "There are ways, Storm," she said at last. "Luke has friends. Dad thinks the world of him. So do the boys."

"And they're prepared to demonstrate that devotion?" Storm asked with barely concealed sarcasm. "When you go home, Carla, with your news, which I haven't the slightest doubt will travel far and wide, you can tell your family I'll never sell Winding River. This is part of *my* heritage. My children will inherit it."

Carla's mouth turned down. "That's a long way off, Storm," she pointed out. "Lots could happen between now and then. Luke may be agonizing over the right thing to do now, but in the end, I believe he'll take up his inheritance. One thing I do know—" she leaned forward, staring directly into Storm's eyes "—whatever power you have over him and I grant you you're beautiful, you'll never turn him into your lackey. He'd rather…"

"Get it all out, Carla," Storm urged, thinking this confrontation was the last thing she needed. "There's something else?"

Some alarm bell went off. "Forgive me," Carla suddenly muttered. "My feelings are running away with me."

"I'd go along with that," Storm answered wryly. "You're a guest in this house, Carla." An uninvited one. She didn't have the heart to mention it.

Carla paled a little. "I'm sorry if you think I've behaved badly, Storm. I have no wish to hurt you. Believe me, I'm your friend."

Storm turned her dark head slowly. "I have a big problem with that."

"All right you're not one of my favourites." Unexpectedly Carla laughed. "You have everything. Money, looks, a career. What I'm really trying to say is lay off Luke."

For an instant Storm felt like crying for them all. Instead she looked out over the drive with its magnificent central fountain. She could hear Noni's footsteps in the hallway coming closer. She was immensely grateful. "Carla," she said quietly, not responding to the other woman's challenge, "I cannot fail to tell you, you've got problems. There's *nothing* between you and Luke except maybe the embers of a friendship. I'm sure under the circumstances you won't want to stay for lunch."

Carla looked back over her shoulder. She too was aware Noni was almost upon them. Noni, the devoted family "friend." "Listen to the lady!" Carla said with a bitter laugh. "I only came to see Luke anyway."

Storm looked up at Carla as she stood swaying like a boxer on her feet. "You surely didn't think I thought otherwise?"

CHAPTER NINE

ONE of the ground staff drove Carla to the airstrip. Storm didn't wave her off. She felt close to collapse. To lose her father, then to have to stabilize her emotions after hearing his will; to consummate her subterranean passion for Luke, to be disabled with her injured ankle. Now Carla with her revelations. It was too much to handle. Surely if Carla were sane she wouldn't continue with her obsessive quest for Luke? Was it possible he continued to encourage her? More likely Carla was a little mad? Not that it wasn't possible to lead a normal life and still obsess about relationships. She wouldn't have believed Carla at all except there was no way Carla could have known. Only three people, four counting Robert, knew the contents of her father's will. Robert, even if he had been in the house, was the soul of discretion. His very livelihood depended upon it. She had only just told Noni. Noni for any number of reasons she ruled out. That left Luke himself.

He and Carla had gone for a walk last night. It was a known fact, at one stage Luke and Carla had been more than friends. Carla when she had no obvious cause of making mischief was good-looking, vivacious, a born country woman with all the necessary skills, and she could be entertaining. Was it possible Luke needed to talk about his life-changing bequest with someone else? Someone he trusted? Luke had to know Carla cared about him deeply. Carla was on *his* side.

Noni coming back into the sunroom where Storm was

167

supposedly resting with her foot up, saw the play of emotions move across Storm's face.

"What an odd girl!" she exclaimed, sinking into an armchair opposite Storm. "One minute she's staying for lunch the next she's off." Noni had been trained to ask questions but she waited.

Storm couldn't help the deep sigh that ran through her, leaving her drained. "You didn't happen to mention anything about Dad's will to her?"

There was a brief awful silence.

"I'm amazed you ask me, Storm," Noni's sweet features registered deep hurt causing Storm's eyes to fill with quick tears.

"Oh, forgive me, Noni. I don't know why I asked. It was a stupid question."

"Except you're not stupid, my girl," Noni pointed out bracingly. "Something was behind it?"

Betrayed? "Carla appears to know just about everything in connection with Luke's inheritance. How Dad left him a half share. How it was a bequest for life. How afterwards it would revert to me or my heirs. Only three of us knew, Noni."

Noni pressed a hand to her head. "You can't possibly think Luke told her?"

There was a bleak expression in Storm's eyes. "They went for a walk last night. I know Luke was shocked by the sheer size of Dad's bequest. Luke can't say everything to me. Maybe he needed to confide in a friend."

But Noni had a talent for sounding out emotions. "Dearest girl, he's *not* in love with Carla. I can tell you that."

"He must have thought he was in love with her at one time?" Storm stared back a little helplessly, looking more vulnerable than Noni had yet seen her. In fact she looked fragile.

"Just as you thought you were in love with Alex and that other fellow," Noni countered reasonably.

"Then how *did* she know, Noni? I don't think I could bear it if I thought Luke had taken her into his confidence. She mentioned something else that was telling about Luke. She said he would never be my lackey."

"He never said that," Noni answered promptly, with scorn.

"Maybe not those words. But he did tell me he wouldn't work for me. That was before the will was read."

Noni was tempted to say what she thought and gave into the temptation. "You're in love with him aren't you?" she said gently.

"*In* love with him?" Storm was almost in tears. "Noni, I love him. I've always loved him. But unthinking, unknowingly, Dad pushed us apart. His latest attempt to bring us together hasn't had much success, either."

Noni knew all the facts; recalled them. "I've watched you two for many long years," she said. "I looked on helplessly while your father, with the best of intentions, did a lot of harm. You *must* accept, Storm, your father loved Luke. Luke was just the sort of boy, the young man your father would have wanted for a son. It affected you badly, but in your father's eyes his love for Luke had nothing to do with his love for you. You were his beautiful, gifted daughter. But in his eyes no woman could be strong enough, exceptional enough to run a cattle empire. The Major wasn't about to throw a lifetime's work away. Or the McFarlane heritage."

"So he devised a scheme whereby Luke and I would marry, little caring if there was fallout?" Storm said, her eyes sad.

"It's up to you, Storm," Noni said, her voice firm but comforting. "Your life has been complicated for so long.

It's time to free yourself of the bonds. Talk to Luke. I'm
sure he'll come up with a perfectly reasonable explanation.''

The muster was ahead of schedule which gave Luke a lot
of satisfaction. Most of the herd was now within a day's
journey of water. He'd been up very early that morning to
greet four of the stockmen coming in from the skeleton
camp where they had spent the night. They were strung
out perhaps a half mile apart, stock-whips cracking, driving the bellowing beasts in the desired direction towards
water. Very soon he'd know where all his cows and calves
were. It was time to delegate a few of his jobs so he could
visit the outstations. He had intended doing that, but the
Major's death had changed everyone's plans.

As always no matter what he was doing his mind drifted
back to Storm. He had taken such delight, such exhilaration in the beauty and passion of their coming together. It
had overwhelmed him so much so he had difficulty dealing
with this business of his half share. Storm, initially
shocked and angry and he didn't blame her, now seemed
to have accepted the situation far better than he could. It
was a great honour, but he had difficulty coming to terms
with the magnitude of it. The magnitude of winning Storm,
like plucking a star from the sky. With a half share in
Winding River, running it as he wanted, he had the world
at his feet. They needed to take in another station. Central
Queensland for preference, not big in Winding River's
terms, but providing lush green feed for at least six months
or so of the year. He had just such a station in mind. The
bulk of the cattle would be straight Brahmin. Storm had a
good mind.

When things settled, perhaps after he had a chance to
visit the outstations, he would discuss it with her. He just

hoped she hadn't been too irritated by Carla's comments and performance last night. Carla's wish to hold onto him seemed almost neurotic. God knows what Carla would think when she got around to hearing the Major had left him a half share in Winding River. She would hear it if he took up his bequest. She would hear it and half the world if either Storm fought the will or he forfeited the bequest. He had come to see Carla had a strange pattern of behaviour. She had gone to considerable lengths last night to make it appear to Storm their short affair was far from over. At the same time she was seeing Les Marshall. Sex was very important to Carla. Les would be sure to oblige.

He returned to the bungalow at dusk, found a little note from Storm asking him to come up to the house for dinner. Noni must have delivered it, he thought, pleased in one way Noni was home, but mindful in another Storm now had a chaperone. No glorious night in Storm's bed. He was still light-headed at the thought of it. He couldn't possibly let her get away. He loved her. Extravagantly. She knew that of course. He had always loved her.

He knew the minute he saw her something was wrong. He had been an excellent student of her every expression, every mood, though she covered up well. Noni ate with them, the meal hour quiet but companionable. Afterwards Noni withdrew to the kitchen, refusing his offer to carry in the dishes.

"I'll pile them all on the trolley, dear." Noni smiled. "You two enjoy the cool of the verandah. I'll bring coffee out shortly."

She allowed herself to be carried, looking absolutely beautiful in a light dress that was the colour of lilacs he supposed. Or maybe jacaranda. Her face was so close to his he wanted to kiss her, his eyes travelling to her mouth as lustrous as a rose. The scent of her intoxicated him. She smelt so delicious, cool even when the temperature soared.

The moon was out with a glittering trail of stars, so close to hand one only had to reach out.

"You've been very quiet," he remarked, after he settled her comfortably in her favourite peacock chair.

"I'm finding it a bit wearing not being able to get about," Storm explained, inside shaking with nerves.

"The swelling is subsiding." He glanced approvingly at her ankle.

"At best I might be right in about another ten days."

Behind Luke's handsome head was the dazzling sky and the moon. She fixed her eyes on it. If only issues didn't constantly present themselves.

"So what's wrong?" he asked when she finally looked back at him. "I suppose it has something to do with Carla?"

"Why would you say that?" She levered herself up a bit, straightening her shoulders.

"Carla suffers from delusions," he drawled. "That was only an act last night. There's nothing between Carla and me. You of all people should know that." How could she not?

She picked up a cushion and held it to her like a child. "Except you do talk to her?"

"About what?" Luke's strong features tensed. Hadn't it always been like this? Why did he allow himself to hope things would be different?

"Oh, Luke!" Storm expelled a long sigh, her beautiful hands working a little. "I know there's a perfectly good explanation?"

"I repeat, about what?" A thousand confrontations crammed his mind.

She looked at his taut face, such an aching in her. "All

right, Carla said you told her in confidence about Dad's will. How you inherited a half share. How it was termed a life estate. How—''

"And you believed her?" He cut her off abruptly.

"Only because there was no other way she could have known." Storm's eyes pleaded with him.

"I bet you told Noni," he said.

"Yes, I did. I love Noni. She loves me. She's been with me since I was a child. I trust her."

"But you don't trust *me*. You'll sleep with me. You lose yourself in my arms. I can arouse you again and again, but it's only sex—a great charge of emotion. Maybe it even makes you feel wicked."

"Luke!" She was shocked to the depths of her soul.

"Who the hell am I anyway?" he demanded. "Just the kid your father took on. The kid left without a father and mother. Hell, you've hated me all your life."

An answering anger flashed through her. "Hate you…hate you…" How she longed to spring up. "I *love* you. I've been ill thinking about all this."

"You love me do you?" He moved towards her like a panther, pinning her face in his hand. "Let's hear your little cry of pleasure." He bent his head and took her mouth, in his fevered state letting his hand shape her breast, feeling the instant swell of the nipple. He kissed her long and hard, as if they were about to be estranged and he wanted her to remember.

"Luke," she whispered. "Please stop." She had to, *had* to beg his forgiveness.

Immediately he stepped back, full of self-loathing. "I don't know how it is or why it is I let you do these things to me. But it's all over, Storm. I won't be your scapegoat for the rest of my life."

Pressing her hands down on the sides of her chair, Storm

managed to stand up, in her agitation putting her injured foot to the floor.

"Aaaah!" She couldn't control the whimper of pain.

He couldn't *not* help her. Even now. He went to her, took her weight, pressing her back into her chair.

"Tomorrow I'm going to visit the outstations," he said in a perfectly hard voice. "I'll be gone probably a week maybe a little more. I'll let you know. I don't know why I'm bothering to tell you this, but I told Carla nothing at all. It would be impossible feeling the way I do... did...about you. But I'm not swallowing your distrust any more. I don't know how Carla came by her information, but I think you might consider Carla is not above snooping."

"That's it!" Storm's knees were trembling. She suddenly remembered the little sound she had heard when she and Noni were talking in the sunroom. "That's it! She overheard me talking to Noni. Oh God, Luke, you must let me apologise."

"Don't bother!" His voice rasped, his eyes like blue fire. "I thought I loved you, Storm. I thought I loved everything about you even your astonishing aberrations. I wanted everything from you. I wanted it all. I wanted to marry you. I wanted you to have our children. I was fool enough to think we could start again with Winding River to be held in trust for the heir who was strong enough to hold it together. But it's over. You've given me too much pain."

Sick with emotion, Storm held out her hands to him. "Don't do this to me now, Luke. You've always been able to forgive me no matter what I've done."

"Not any more." He looked around him blindly, hardly seeing anything for his upset. "I've known no other home but here on Winding River. It's time now to move on."

*   *   *

It was the longest ten days Storm had ever known. She filled in her time as best she could, working on her collection—the ideas weren't coming—replying to Sara who had sent her a long, loving letter from Rome, where the news of Athol McFarlane's death had reached her; replying to innumerable sympathy cards; replying to Alex who had been told of her father's death on his return from Hong Kong. Alex wanted to come and visit her.

"I'll throw up my job if I have to," he told her. "I just want to be by your side."

She thanked him for his genuine expressions of sympathy and his many kindnesses to her, but told him at this sad time she needed to be on her own.

The only tiny ray of sunshine was the fact she was able to put her foot to the ground. Could in fact walk on it. She had mended well. She confided in Noni how Luke had reacted—in any case Noni had guessed something had gone terribly wrong—so both women were feeling powerfully disturbed. Luke had become the linchpin in their existence. Recognising he could go out of their lives left them with feelings of acute depression.

Storm agonized over how she could put things right. Possible courses of action seemed to occupy her mind every single hour of the day and into the night. She simply couldn't envision a life without Luke. Her entire happiness hinged on his being there. She was part of him and he was part of her. Now their alienation made her feel terribly isolated. How very easy it was, she now discovered, to realise the worth of a loved one when the loved one decided to go his own way. It probably wasn't even unusual in relationships but it always came as a great shock. Why hadn't she heeded the warnings? It seemed her time of grace had finally run out.

Luke had left word when he arrived on Duranji,

Outstation One, and when he left. There was a great sense
of relief that the days were passing and soon he would be
coming home.

Home.

It struck Storm cruelly it was just as Luke had said. He
had always *lived* on Winding River but it had never been
his home. It was up to her to change that. Her task was to
get them started on a new life. That's if he would ever
forgive her. Knowing Luke she had to consider seriously
that once he had made a decision he would stick to it.
Winding River had been a battlefield far too long. Outstation Two, Mungin, was more remote, two hundred miles
to the northwest. Luke arrived at the designated time, took
off at a designated time. His inspections were complete.
He would arrive on Winding River around 3:00 p.m. that
Friday afternoon. Over an hour and a half later, Bill
Davidson, the head stockman came up to the homestead a
worried man. Luke's flight was overdue, when Luke was
a man who stuck to his schedule. Bill had already contacted Mungin only to be told everything had been fine
when Luke left. If he had kept to his flight plan he should
have landed on Winding River.

"The weather was brilliantly fine when he left," Bill
was saying. "Scorchingly hot!" No electrical storms in
the area predicted. "Of course he could have put down for
some reason or other," Bill continued, looking anxiously
at Storm for some kind of agreement. Storm, however, felt
such a clutch of fear it was like her heart had seized up.
Bill continued to ramble on, as though talking was a relief,
his forehead furrowed with all sorts of anxieties. Storm
vaguely heard him say something about the automatic distress signal. It hadn't been picked up. Both knew, none
better, how many lives had been lost in light aircraft
crashes throughout the Outback.

The sunset was glorious, turning the riverine desert to a land of molten gold. But for once Storm didn't feel her heart lift at the spectacle. The imperial sun sank behind the great pyramids of fiery red sand dunes. The brief lilac dusk set in with thousands of birds flying into the billabongs in multi-coloured clouds. Somehow Storm had come to grips with her tearing panic. Air Services Australia Search and Rescue was informed, Storm giving all necessary information, her voice falsely calm. Controlling the tone and speed of her delivery helped her keep sane. No radio contact had been made by Luke. Neither could he be reached by radio. No distress signal had been picked up. Search and Rescue had the flight path, which would make the task of finding Luke, and his aircraft less difficult but these occasions were always time for worry. Full-scale operations would begin at first light.

It was going to be a long, long night for everyone on Winding River. There had been plenty of drama over the years. They all had their memories of the Major. But Luke was *young*. Someone special. Nothing could happen to Luke. Station people relied very heavily on each other for support and comfort. Storm turned to Noni at this anxious time. Both of them far too uneasy to think they could find a few hours oblivion in sleep, but both women tried very hard to keep their emotions under control. There was always the possibility of total electrical failure. Luke would have to make a forced landing. He would have to find a clear space to use as a runway. There was a whole inland out there. Mulga country. Spinifex country. Desert. There wasn't much leeway for making a mistake. The only comfort was, Luke was an experienced pilot.

He loved flying with a passion. It was an immense exhilaration. The twin engines roaring into life, soaring into the blue. He loved the colour blue. He supposed everyone had a colour they loved best. Blue was the sky. Blue was peace and freedom. The vast ancient land drifted by beneath him scorched a fiery red by a million suns. It was a wonderful feeling to know he was part of it, this great sun-baked land with its ancient plateaus and its isolated mesas. He rejoiced in the connection. Beneath him lay the desert; the Dead Heart credited with many deaths. Explorers, pioneers, pastoralists, later day tourists who for reasons he could never understand didn't heed the warnings. Some came from a world where there was abundant water everywhere. Down there water was the difference between life and fearsome death.

Up here in the cobalt-blue sky his mind always seemed clearer. Perhaps it was because he was totally alone with his thoughts and the simple exultation of flight. As always during these past, heat filled, hectic days he had been wrestling with what he was going to do with his future. The disabling truth was he could not contemplate a future without Storm in it. No escape for him, he thought wryly. His love for Storm was a raging fever that might never be cured.

The Cessna had been cruising as smoothly as a Rolls-Royce so it came as a tremendous jolt to see his entire instrument panel shut down. Total electrical failure. That meant he had lost all communication. Battery? Choke in the fuel pipe? His mind hit on two likely possibilities. Things happened despite regular maintenance. The twin engines were still humming efficiently but he had no other option than to make a forced landing. And as quickly as possible. He dropped altitude descending to a height where he could search for a reasonably safe landing strip. In this area larger than the United Kingdom there were no highways to hand. No dirt roads. No grassy paddocks. No nice, helpful people. Plenty of mulga country. Spinifex country. Blood-red sand. A land majestic but frightening in its ruggedness. He was well off course before he spotted a wide sandy flat that was dotted with golden spinifex in seed. That would have to be it. He turned downwind in preparation for the landing.

A few hairy moments coming in to land, the spears of the spinifex scratching the undercarriage, the gnarled and twisted trunk of a mulga almost clipping a wing. A desert oak loomed up and for a few heart-stopping moments when his whole life seemed to rush by, he wondered if the Cessna would stop in time.

It did and he swore aloud in his relief.

Once on the ground he looked around him with an awe he had never lost. The immensity, the great silence, the unmistakeable brooding challenge thrilled him, fired his imagination.

I am the desert. I am the Dreaming Place. I will still be here when man is no more.

The landscape was so highly coloured it almost hurt his eyes. Ancient pottery baked hard. He had the shivery feeling he might easily have been the first white man to ever have looked upon it. This was forbidding country for anyone who didn't know it intimately. The sun at its peak generated temperatures of more than forty-three degrees. Ally that to the excessively dry atmosphere, and a man could dehydrate within forty-eight hours, leaving a mummified corpse. He always carried water without fail. He was a skilled bushman. He had lived in this environment all his life. He had learned well at the feet of the tribal elders. He knew where to dig for water. He knew what plants to eat. He *could* survive but he was pitted against the cruellest environment in the world. The desert.

Surrounded by so much primordial splendour he felt no

fear. He wasn't going to perish. Maybe it would take time but Air Rescue would find him. Besides he had to live to tell that woman, that Storm McFarlane, he was going to marry her. There wasn't anything she was going to be able to do about it, either. He knew her mind better than she did.

He turned to make his inspection of the Cessna, discovering like he thought the problem was battery melt down. In the near distance he could see a family of dingoes on the prowl, ears pricked, at the alert. Further off a couple of camels were running wild and his mind harked back to the day he had saved the Major's life. Even now he could feel the Major's strong hand on his shoulder, hear the deep rumble of his voice:

You stood your ground in the face of fear. I promise you I won't forget it.

He had saved the Major's life. Now it had come to him his destiny was to give his daughter the best possible life. To love her and involve her in all his plans. She had such energy in life. So had he. They needed to combine it for the future. For their children. For Winding River. By now she would have learned the news. He hadn't turned up on the station. Communication lines had been broken. He knew in his heart she would be desolate if anything happened to him. If nothing else, they had to get their love out into the open. Once settled they could work together to find answers.

So heartened, with the vision of Storm very clear in his mind, Luke went about the job of preparing to spend the night in a desert where the great heat of the day would drop to a comparative freezing.

It had been a terrible night for both of them. By midmorning they still had not received word, though they all clung to hope. A full-scale search was in operation. The downed aircraft would be spotted. Luke would be safe and well.

Thirty hours. Thirty minutes. Forty seconds. Storm thought. All that morning in torment. It was like living with a knife in her breast. To have parted in such anger! It was more than she could bear. Why had they spent so much time in arguing? More to the point why had she? All their lives it was Luke who had shown the understanding, the tolerance. She, especially vulnerable as a girl child then a young woman, had railed against Luke's position in her father's life. For this maybe her father was to blame but she was old enough now to get her futile hang-ups under control. She would do anything, be anything, give all her money away, to have Luke safely back in her arms.

Driven by emotion the anguish that would never empty out until Luke was safely home, Storm gathered branches of white bauhinias in flower from the home grounds; sheaves of the sun-loving zinnias and masses of greenery taking the Jeep to Sanctuary Hill. Of course the flowers couldn't possibly survive, not in the heat, but her grief directed her to strip the orchid trees and pile up the gorgeous open-faced zinnias that flowered profusely even in the dry.

Once at the cemetery, Storm lay her floral offerings first on her parents' graves. They lay side by side. She moved a distance away, past her ancestors' graves with their monumental headstones to where Luke's parents had been laid to rest. Again side by side as husband and wife should be. The white bauhinia branches she lay on the graves of the women, the mothers. The multicoloured zinnias she strew over the graves of her father and Luke's. How the lives of the two families had been intermingled. How could she possibly let Luke leave when his parents were here on

Sanctuary Hill? It was unthinkable. All her life she had been afraid to trust. But it wasn't too late. Dear God, don't let it be too late. Storm bent her head and prayed with the greatest intensity she had known in her life. Prayed that Luke would be found safe and uninjured. She prayed all the old hurts would go away. The love she had for Luke couldn't disappear into a void. She prayed for her family. She prayed for Luke's family. Unwilling to leave this strangely peaceful spot, she was forced to seek shelter beneath the magnificent desert oak that grew near the entrance. Sanctuary Hill was surrounded on all sides by a tall wrought-iron fence with double wrought-iron gates hung from stone pillars to lock it in.

Another scorching day and Luke was out there in the desert. Even with the shelter of the wing the heat would be intense. She knew he would be carrying that precious commodity water. None of them travelled any distance into the desert country without it. Worn-out by her sleepless night and the crushing weight of anxiety Storm allowed her lids to fall…

A voice somewhere spoke her name. She was dreaming. It was Luke. The tears started up behind her shut eyelids. The bond between them was so strong he could reach her even in sleep.

The hand moved from her wrist to her face, stroking, caressing, the voice repeating her name.

"Storm…Storm!" So much love in it. Longing. Concern. Her splendid white knight.

"Darling, everything's all right. You can open your eyes. I'm here. I'm really here."

Maybe the dream was playing a cruel joke. He *wasn't* really there. But strong arms reached for her. Flesh and bone. She was drawn to her feet. Those same arms locked themselves around her like they would never, never, let her go. Not even in eternity.

She lifted her head and stared straight into Luke's blazing blue eyes. They were all the more jewel-like because his eyes, like hers, glittered with tears.

"Luke! Oh thank you, God!" She sagged against him overcome by relief and joy, unable to say any more because he lowered his head; kissed her with such a flame of passion it burned itself into her. "I couldn't go on without you," she told him emotionally when he allowed her breath. "I love you with all my heart."

"As I love you," he answered immediately, voice vibrant with emotion. "I could never go away and leave you. I could never die without telling you, you're all the magic, all the wonder in my life."

"Can you forgive me?" she beseeched him, touching his beloved face with a wondering hand.

He shook his gleaming dark red head. "There'll be no talk of forgiveness between us. The old days are past. What we're going to talk about endlessly is our future. You and me. I want you to marry me, Storm. I want it as soon as it's respectful to your father. I want you to be my wife, the mother of my children. I want us to be together in this life and the next. I want when the time comes, a long, long way off, we'll lie here side by side. Maybe our daughter will come to cover us with blossoms. White as a bridal veil. Marry me, Storm. I won't take no for an answer."

She hugged his lean body to her, her hands digging into his hard-muscled back. "I'll marry you. I promise. I wish it were tomorrow but I think it must be April. April is a lovely month. Would you like an April bride?" she asked radiantly.

He gathered her to him; held her right up to his heart. "April is perfect. Heaven. I can't wait to see you in your bridal finery walking towards me."

EPILOGUE

APRIL IN THE CHANNEL COUNTRY
THE MIRACLE OF THE WILD FLOWERS
THE BRANAGAN-McFARLANE WEDDING

The Branagan-McFarlane wedding celebrated on historic Winding River Station received wide coverage in the press. It was an open secret the stunningly handsome bridegroom, the late Major Athol McFarlane's protégé had received a half share in the famous station in recognition of his services to the family but that seemed neither here nor there when the bridegroom was to continue running the McFarlane operation as he had in the past. It was reported the happy couple was to make the station their home although the bride, an acclaimed jewellery designer would continue her career selling her beautiful pieces through favoured outlets.

Three hundred guests had been invited to the wedding. They came from all over the country and overseas. A famous women's magazine was allowed coverage on the understanding the substantial fee in the form of a cheque would be made out to the Sydney Children's Hospital, a charity dear to the bride's heart. Everyone who attended the wedding could speak of nothing else for months on end. The floodwaters the station had received during the Wet had receded leaving a wonderland of wildflowers on a gigantic scale. Flowers to the horizon! A total transformation of the desert landscape; millions and millions of everlastings holding up their pretty paper faces, white, yellow and pink, the fluffy flowered mulla-mulla, the crimson of the desert peas, the masses and masses of other wildflowers that traced their coloured embroidery across the vast land. It was a sight no guest, especially those who had never witnessed such a miracle, were likely to forget.

And the homestead! Glorious! The bride had refurbished it. What exquisite taste! The wedding ceremony was held in the old ballroom where everyone got quite teary at the obvious love that bathed the happy couple in radiance. The beauty of the bride was a great talking point. Her gown was *fabulous!* Strapless with a romantic billowing skirt of ivory delustred satin, the hem and some twelve inches of the grand traditional skirt, like some primitively inspired piece of jewellery, were encrusted with various coloured beads, brilliants and crystals, in an amazingly beautiful aboriginal motif.

The bride's lustrous mane of dark hair was drawn back from the face but allowed to cascade down her back. She wore the traditional long bridal veil simply caught so as not to detract from the quite wonderful piece of jewellery she wore around her throat. A combination of stones her adoring bridegroom had found for her since childhood, sapphires and opals, mixed up with precious and semiprecious jewels. It was extraordinary and it added the drama quite in keeping with the bride's vivid style of beauty. The bride had four attendants and two flower girls, twins. All of them looked lovely on the big day, the enchanting little girls modelling silk representations of the station's wildflowers, as diadems on their golden curls.

It was all so passionate, so rife with promise; the

guests were quite carried away by the emotion of it all.
The bridegroom was described at every turn as "simply
smashing." An understatement in the eyes of his deliriously happy bride.

As one important family dowager was later heard to
remark as she watched Luke and Storm whirling through
their wedding waltz. "Those two are soul mates! Just
look at the expression of love on their faces. It's so
transparent it gives me goose bumps. Mark my words—
which everyone did—this is a marriage that will last!"

She said it again at the family christening some eighteen months later. Storm and Luke gave a big party to
celebrate the birth of their first child, the most gorgeous,
the most adorable little girl child. The child had her
father's hair; perhaps a couple of shades more to rosy-
red. At six weeks old she didn't have the expected navy
eyes. Emily's eyes were a clear beautiful green. Could
anything be more perfect?

SINGLE IN THE CITY...

English heiresses Annis and Bella are as
different as sisters can be. Annis is clever
and quiet, Bella beautiful and bubbly.
Yet with a millionaire father, they both think
they'll never find a man who wants them
for *themselves*....

How wrong can they be!

Don't miss this fabulous duet by rising star

Sophie Weston

THE MILLIONAIRE'S DAUGHTER
January 2002 #3683

THE BRIDESMAID'S SECRET
February 2002 #3687

in

Harlequin Romance®

HARLEQUIN®
Makes any time special ®

Visit us at www.eHarlequin.com   HRWESTON

If you enjoyed what you just read,
then we've got an offer you can't resist!

Take 2 bestselling love stories FREE!

Plus get a FREE surprise gift!

Harlequin Romance®

CALL THE ONES YOU LOVE OVER THE HOLIDAYS!

Save $25 off future book purchases when you buy any four Harlequin® or Silhouette® books in October, November and December 2001,

PLUS

receive a phone card good for 15 minutes of long-distance calls to anyone you want in North America!

WHAT AN INCREDIBLE DEAL!

Just fill out this form and attach 4 proofs of purchase (cash register receipts) from October, November and December 2001 books, and Harlequin Books will send you a coupon booklet worth a total savings of $25 off future purchases of Harlequin® and Silhouette® books, AND a 15-minute phone card to call the ones you love, anywhere in North America.

Please send this form, along with your cash register receipts as proofs of purchase, to:

In the USA: Harlequin Books, P.O. Box 9057, Buffalo, NY 14269-9057
In Canada: Harlequin Books, P.O. Box 622, Fort Erie, Ontario L2A 5X3
Cash register receipts must be dated no later than December 31, 2001.
Limit of 1 coupon booklet and phone card per household.
Please allow 4-6 weeks for delivery.

**I accept your offer! Enclosed are 4 proofs of purchase.
Please send me my coupon booklet
and a 15-minute phone card:**

Name: _____

Address: _____ City: _____

State/Prov.: _____ Zip/Postal Code: _____

Account Number (if available): _____

---

097 KJB DAGL
PHQ4013